安陸 ◎ 著

拯救 你的 英檢聽力！

四週 勇闖 英語檢定

別再對自己的英檢聽力見死不救！

- 每次英檢都敗在聽力？
- 考試抓不到關鍵字？
- 英文常常有聽沒有懂？
- 英文聽懂了卻不知道要怎麼回？
- 覺得該加強聽力，卻不知從何下手？
  其實你沒有菜英文，你只是不知道該怎麼用！

就差那臨門一腳了！

本書為讀者們精心規劃四週課程，一週五天，每天兩小時，搭配四大章節【看圖辨義篇】、【朗讀特訓篇】、【看圖敘述篇】、【問答特訓篇】，由美籍外師專業錄音的光碟，透過看圖、懂圖、解圖，延伸相關敘述答案，教你如何聽、如何解、如何答，只要短短一個月就輕鬆穩拿英檢聽力高分！

從此考聽力不再吃鱉！

MP3

作者序及簡介

　　某較為嚴格的航空公司將空服人員的英語甄選標準設定為中高級以上亦即多益成績必須是 750 分以上才符合應徵資格。此航空公司曾聘用一位多益分數高達八百分以上的空姐但上班了半年後，卻發現她不僅外籍乘客的英語聽不懂，自己所能與乘客交談的內容也僅只是"COFFEE? TEA?"，結果也引來一些輕佻的人在後面加上兩個字"OR ME?"來揶揄她（連起來就是「你要咖啡、茶、還是我？」），鬧得機艙裡又是訕笑又是尷尬。在座艙長的詢問之下才發現她的分數都是補習班補出來的，補習班就是有一套讓人得分的高招，但是一到現實生活那些分數就不管用了。這位空服員所謂的八百多分就是早年只以聽與讀為主的測驗成績，現在多益加考了說與寫，但不像全民英檢必須聽說讀寫四項全合格才算一級通過。

　　類似空服員這樣考試成績與現實生活應用出現落差的情形，早年在赴美留學生中也很常見的，許多傳統托福將近滿分（相當於英檢的高級）的學生，到了美國校園仍然聽不懂也說不出口，後來新托福測聽說讀寫，也是由於發現只測聽與讀所產生的問題。而一次測完四項語言技能，似乎較符合語言的天性。

　　目前全民英檢測驗的順序是先測聽說再測讀寫，應試者在準備考試的過程中，須熟練應試技巧，但仍與實際情境產生脫節。學生在急於先通過聽與讀的考試壓力下，疏於練習說與寫，而且是在通過初試後一年內再找時間練習說與寫。這其實是違反人類語言生成天性的。當今英語教學泰斗道格拉斯‧布朗(H. Douglas Brown)在聽力理解教學上特重互動(Interaction)，特別是問答與會話這兩部份「在聽解過程中免不了會產生互動現象。會話特別與互動有密切關係，舉凡協商、澄清、引起注意、輪流，或是主題的提出、維持與結束，全都是互動的。考生即使熟練了應試技巧考了高分，終究還是難以把所學靈活運用在現實生活中。

因此編這本書的目的，除了希望能幫助急於要考英檢的學者，兼顧他在實際生活上的靈活運用，你第一眼看到的就是全真的試題，然後我們針對這些題目所提供的語料進行模擬問答、會話互動，再進一部分析這些語料的字彙、文法的運用，讓你一步一步都踏在真實考與用的情境中，既熟悉題型，又熟悉用法。

　　既然我們強調的是互動，就不能只是讀者與書的互動，而是隨著錄音檔中所引導的活動練習，先是機械式的練習困難的字彙語句，然後必須把學會的語句用在與真人的交談上，學者可以二人結伴或三人以上編組，隨著書上設計的活動，自己另創造類似話題或文法句型的對話，把現實生活中可能面臨的難題拿出來與同伴一起解決，減少像前述空姐那樣的困境。

常安陸

編者序

　　大家最熟悉的英檢考法莫過於聽力和閱讀，相信很多人都有過這樣的困擾，聽力考試相對簡單，但是實際碰到英文母語人士可能得多花些時間理解他們的口語，或是聽得懂對方說什麼，可是自己卻搭不上半句英文。本書規劃了四週結合英文聽力與口說的訓練課程，透過每天週一至週五的練習和週末的複習，讓讀者聽說能力躍進，除了於各類英語檢定考試中能過關斬將，也能實際應用到日常生活中。

編輯群

拯救你的英檢聽力！

四週課程勇闖英語檢定

目　次

WEEK ① 看圖辨義篇

WEEK ② 朗讀特訓篇

WEEK ③ 看圖敘述篇

四週課程勇闖英語檢定

	Week 1	Week 2	Week 3	Week 4
Day 1				
Day 2				
Day 3				
Day 4				
Day 5				
Day 6	review	review	review	review
Day 7	review	review	review	review

WEEK 1

看圖辨義篇

WEEK **1** 看圖辨義篇

我們先介紹英檢題型的「看圖辨義」與多益「圖片敘述」的模擬聽力測驗的差異與答題技巧，然後再說明如何把聽解技巧運用在口說技巧上。

英檢的圖以測驗的主題繪製，大致分為情境、位置、天氣、職業、價格、流程、動作、比較、發音等，因此一張圖考一至三題不等，可以從不同的目的考同一張圖。而多益則是一張照片只考一題，大致分為人物與靜物兩種，測驗重點為基本字彙、動詞與介系詞，其句型多為「主詞＋動詞＋受詞」，而且絕不會考背景的細節。要注意其混淆的選項 (distracters)，概分意義、發音或意義加發音等三類。設計於誤導位置、環境、空間安排、動作、面部表情、肢體語言、外貌特徵、認知物件、景物存在人物、材質、人物與背景細節等。

而這些問法也正是我們稍後延伸口語問答、對話、敘述的口說基礎。因此我們做多益聽力測驗時，就要提示每題的混淆目的與答題技巧，從模仿複誦母語人士的發音，進一步理解敘述的技巧就是答題技巧，為口說練習建立好正確觀念。

我們探討聽力答題技巧的目的不只是在聽力測驗上可以拿高分，

更是要為以後練習「看圖敘述」做好準備，所以會強調有益於口說的技巧分析。事實上，任何教導增強聽力的課本都會建議，要考好聽力測驗最好的辦法還是多練習口說，只有從模仿熟習母語的發音（包含其口音、變音）特質，才能容易聽懂他們的發音。也只有多以口說熟習單字、片語、文法的運用，才能更容易聽懂這些單字、片語與文法。

　　回答聽力測驗的第一要務就是爭取預判 (prediction) 的時間，不能等待聽完題目才去看圖片，這樣每題都可能還沒做，下一題又來了。預判的方法，我們區分幾個重點：

1. 對圖片上的人物，要注意：
   A. 他們在做甚麼 (what) ？在哪裡 (where) ？
   B. 他們是誰 (who) ？是否穿甚麼制服或拿甚麼工具顯示他們的身份。
   C. 如何區別他們 (what) ？ 注意有無特殊的服飾、髮型、眼鏡、帽子等等。
   D. 表情如何 (how) ？ 喜怒哀樂等等。
2. 對圖片上的靜物，要注意：那是甚麼東西 (what) ？甚麼材質 (what is it made of) ？在做甚麼？以及在甚麼地方等等。
3. 對圖片上的場景，注意：在哪裡？ 前方 (in front of) 有甚麼？ 發生甚麼事了？ 其背景（圖片遠後方有甚麼）等等。
4. 注意其混淆的選項 (distracters)，有三大類：
   A. 發音的混淆：如 project 與 reject ；aware「察覺」與 wear「穿戴」可以是近似音混淆。

B. 意義的混淆：如 research「研究」與 search「搜尋」二者音也相近，但個別的對象不同，當然意思也不同。

C. 發音與意義的混淆：如 "It rains cats and dogs"（大雨滂沱）與"He raises cats and dogs"（他養貓與狗）。二者音近，意卻完全不同。

5. 上述預判項目中所涉及可能的字彙片語，如站在一大片湖或河水前面，就該聯想到 watching, water, river, lake, scenery… 等等的字彙。

　　大部分的正確答案都是現在簡單式或現在進行式，小心其他時態的選項。

　　此外再補充有關口語體該注意的，有些是平日要多多記誦的，有許多幾乎是字面意思無法理解的，如"He has a sweet tooth"（他愛吃甜食）；"he is under weather"（他不舒服）等等包括成語 (idioms)、俚語 (slang)、簡化語、特殊風俗民情等等，不論是獨白或對話都常出現，當然考試就少不了它們。由於不熟習俗語的學生會對字面上意義的誤解，在答案選項中就會有以字面解釋的選項來混淆，例如這題 The new novel in the bookstore is selling like hot cakes. 選項中就可以拿 hot, cake, 甚至 cookies 來混淆：

A. Perhaps we should go on a cooler day.

B. So, how do you like the cake?

C. You mean he ate all of the cookies?

　　在熟習了聽力作答要領後，大家想想，如果換成問你問題的是一個真人，你是否還是必須以這些要領看著圖去回答呢？同樣的，問的人是否也會以這些重點去問對方呢？這樣，我們從複誦聽力考題去延伸的口說技巧就跟著成熟了，那時你會發現，全民英檢的看圖口說測驗與看圖聽解的問題其實是一樣的，那時你在準備口說測驗上也就已經駕輕就熟了。

　　我們體驗一下模擬的多益聽力測驗「圖片描述」(Picture Description)，多益與英檢不同的是，每題一張圖片，錄音內容為四個選項，考生須從其中選出最符合圖片的描述。現在請大家打開音檔，一起先做這十題第一部份。

Picture Description

Look and choose the statement that best describes what you see in the picture. Mp3 001

1.

2.

3.

4.

5.

6.

7.

8.

9.

10.

核對答案：

1. B　2. D　3. A　4. C　5. B　6. B　7. D　8. B　9. B　10. B

　　接下來再播放 **1-10** 題一遍，隨著音軌的播放，找同伴練習問答，練習時甲同學按下列問題內容問乙同學，乙同學回答正確答案。注意！盡量模仿母語人士的口音、音調以及不同情境所表現的情感，乙同學此時已經知道該選的答案，所以要特別注意聽要回答的選項。

甲播放 ABCD 四選項，每播完一項暫停，再複誦：

1. (A) There are two signs near the tree.

　(B) The sign is behind the tree.

　(C) This tree has a bell on it.

　(D) No trees can be seen in the court.

　乙回答：(B) The sign is behind the tree.

> 預判出現的字彙有：
> Sign, tree, court, lamp, parasol, behind, near 等。

甲個別播放 ABCD 四選項，每播完一項暫停，再複誦：

2. (A) The man is walking beside the car.

   (B) There are hundreds of cars on the street.

   (C) The man is wearing a shirt.

   (D) Some tattoos can be seen on the man's back.

   乙回答：(D) Some tattoos can be seen on the man's back.

   > 預判出現的字彙有：
   > Car, motorcycle, street, topless, shirtless, tattoos, bare-chested, behind 等。

甲個別播放 ABCD 四選項，每播完一項暫停，再複誦：

3. (A) The roof is planted with flowers.

   (B) Three poles are at the bottom of the roof.

   (C) The people are far away from the roof.

   (D) The day is sunny.

   > 預判出現的字彙有：roof, flower, poles, crowds, cloudy, on the top of, under 等。

   乙回答：(A) The roof is planted with flowers.

甲個別播放 ABCD 四選項，每播完一項暫停，再複誦：

4. (A) There are a trio of dancers on the stage.

   (B) All of them are in black.

   (C) The audience is paying attention to the performance.

   (D) They are all playing rings in front of the audience.

   乙回答：(C) The audience is paying attention to the performance.

   > 預判出現的字彙有：dancers, stage, audience, performance, ring, 等。

播音內容

1. (A) There are two signs near the tree.
   (B) The sign is behind the tree.
   (C) This tree has a bell on it.
   (D) No trees can be seen in the court.

解析：	(A) 樹的附近有兩個招牌。
文句以靜物的空間安置為誤導，所以有 near, behind, on, in 等的介系詞表達各項物件的位置。此外有物件的誤導如 bell，有與無的誤導如 There is no... 等。	(B) 招牌在樹的後面。
	(C) 樹上有一隻鈴鐺。
	(D) 庭院裡沒有一棵樹。

2. (A) The man is walking beside the car.
   (B) There are hundreds of cars on the street.
   (C) The man is wearing a shirt.
   (D) Some tattoos can be seen on the man's back.

解析：	(A) 那人走在那輛車旁邊。
(A) 以靜物的空間安置為誤導，(B)(C) 為物件的誤導。	(B) 有數百輛汽車在大街上。
	(C) 這個人穿著一件襯衫。
	(D) 這個人的背上可以看出一些紋身。

3. (A) The roof is planted with flowers.

(B) Three poles are at the bottom of the roof.

(C) The people are far away from the roof.

(D) The day is sunny.

解析：	(A) 屋頂上種著花草。
(B) (C) 以靜物的空間安置為誤導，(D) 為環境的誤導。	(B) 三根旗桿在屋頂的底部。
	(C) 人群離屋頂很遠。
	(D) 這一天是晴天。

4. (A) There are a trio of dancers on the stage.

(B) All of them are in black.

(C) The audience is paying attention to the performance.

(D) They are all playing rings in front of the audience.

解析：	(A) 有三個舞者在舞臺上。
(A) 以 a trio of（三人一組）的片語考驗聽者的片語能力來辨識背景的認知。(B) 人物衣服色彩的誤導。(D) 其他人物細節的觀察。	(B) 他們都穿黑色。
	(C) 聽眾注意的看表演。
	(D) 他們都在觀眾面前表演輪環。

甲個別播放 ABCD 四選項，每播完一項暫停，再複誦：

5. (A) The woods are near the river.

(B) The bridge is in the middle of water.

(C) There is no passengers in the center of the bridge.

(D) There is a weeping willow on top of the bridge.

乙回答：(B) The bridge is in the middle of water.

> 預判出現的字彙有：water, river, lake, woods, willows, bridge, in the middle of 等。

甲個別播放 ABCD 四選項，每播完一項暫停，再複誦：

6. (A) This is a toy crane.

(B) This is a real crane.

(C) This is a statue of a crane.

(D) This is a crane in the air.

乙回答：(B) This is a real crane.

> 預判出現的字彙有：crane, fence, wire, bird 等。

甲個別播放 ABCD 四選項，每播完一項暫停，再複誦：

7. (A) Three rhinos are playing under the shade.

(B) There are no trees around the rhinos.

(C) They are walking around the yard.

(D) Two of the rhinos are sleeping.

乙回答：(D) Two of the rhinos are sleeping.

> 預判出現的字彙有：rhino, yard, sleep, bushes, trees 等。

甲個別播放 ABCD 四選項，每播完一項暫停，再複誦：

8. (A) The bridge is on the top of mountains.

   (B) The bridge stretches across the stream.

   (C) The stream is close by the bridge.

   (D) The bridge is at the end of the valley.

   乙回答：(B) The bridge stretches across the stream.

預判出現的字彙有：bridge, mountains, stream, valley, on the top of, above, under 等。

【Day 1】
Monday

播音內容

5. (A) The woods are near the river.

   (B) The bridge is in the middle of water.

   (C) There is no passengers in the center of the bridge.

   (D) There is a weeping willow on top of the bridge.

解析：	(A) 樹林在河的附近。
文句以靜物的空間安置為誤導，所以有 near, in the middle of, in the center, on top of 等的介系詞片語來表達各項物件的位置。	(B) 這座橋在水中央。 (C) 這座橋的中心沒有遊客。 (D) 一棵垂柳在這座橋的橋頂。

6. (A) This is a toy crane.

   (B) This is a real crane.

   (C) This is a statue of a crane.

   (D) This is a crane in the air.

解析：	(A) 這是一種玩具鶴。
(A) (C) 涉及了材質的判斷，(D) 則是背景的誤導。	(B) 這是一個真正的鶴。
	(C) 這是一隻鶴的雕像。
	(D) 在空中有一隻鶴。

7. (A) Three rhinos are playing under the shade.
　 (B) There are no trees around the rhinos.
　 (C) They are walking around the yard.
　 (D) <u>Two of the rhinos are sleeping.</u>

解析：	(A) 三隻犀牛正在樹蔭下玩。
(A) (C) 誤導圖中動物的活動。	(B) 犀牛周圍沒有樹。
(B) 是背景的誤導。	(C) 它們在院子裡散步。
	(D) 兩個犀牛在睡覺。

8. (A) The bridge is on the top of mountains.
　 (B) <u>The bridge stretches across the stream.</u>
　 (C) The stream is close by the bridge.
　 (D) The bridge is at the end of the valley.

解析：	(A) 這座橋在山頂上。
文句以靜物的空間安置為誤導，所以有 on the top of, close by, at the end of, 等的介系詞片語來表達各項物件的位置。	(B) 這座橋橫跨溪流。
	(C) 溪流貼近那座橋。
	(D) 這座橋在山谷盡頭。

甲個別播放 ABCD 四選項，每播完一項暫停，再複誦：

9. (A) Some passengers are ready to jump.

(B) The suspension bridge has a red tower.

(C) One of the passengers is under the suspension bridge.

(D) No passenger is passing the suspension bridge.

乙回答：(B) The suspension bridge has a red tower.

預判出現的字彙有：suspension bridge, passengers, tower, under 等。

甲個別播放 ABCD 四選項，每播完一項暫停，再複誦：

10. (A) The swans are flying.

(B) The swans are following the ducks.

(C) They are fighting on the lake.

(D) They are sitting in a circle.

乙回答：(B) The swans are following the ducks.

預判出現的字彙有：swans, lake, duck, under, suspension bridge 等。

播音內容

9. (A) Some passengers are ready to jump.	
(B) The suspension bridge has a red tower.	
(C) One of the passengers is under the suspension bridge.	
(D) No passenger is passing the suspension bridge.	
解析：	(A) 一些遊客準備跳下。
(A) 誤導圖中人物的活動。(B)	(B) 這吊橋有一個紅色的橋塔。
(D) 為背景細節的觀察。	(C) 有一個乘客在吊橋下。
	(D) 沒有乘客通過吊橋。

10. (A) The swans are flying.
    (B) The swans are following the ducks.
    (C) They are fighting on the lake.
    (D) They are sitting in a circle.

解析：	(A) 天鵝正在飛翔。
(A) (C) 誤導圖中動物的活動。	(B) 天鵝們跟隨著鴨子。
(D) 為背景細節的觀察。	(C) 他們在湖上打鬥。
	(D) 他們坐在圓圈內。

初步檢討

　　如果一開始接受聽力測驗，你就覺得很難，你的問題就必須朝「造成聽力困難的因素」檢討，去找解決之道。前述我們提到語言教學泰斗道格拉斯・布朗 (H. Douglas Brown) 強調聽與說的互動性，而缺乏互動性是造成聽力理解的阻礙之一。布朗博士在聽力理解教學上，歸納出來八個「可能嚴重阻礙聽力理解」的口語特徵，分別是互動性 (interaction)、群組法 (clustering)、贅語 (redundancy)、簡化詞語 (reduced forms)、表達的變項 (performance variables)、口語體 (colloquial languages)、說話速度 (rate of delivery)、重音、以及節奏與語調 (stress, rhythm and intonation) 等[1]，現在就這八種因素，以筆者多年來教學的經驗，來看看台灣學生所面臨這八項障礙時所反應的特質，也許有助於讀者發現自己的障礙特質。

---

[1] 原則導向的教學法，317-321 頁，施玉惠等譯，東華，台北，2003。

1. 溝通性的：

　　從溝通性的原則上，首先我們要釐清這八項因素並不只是你考英檢成績不好的障礙，而是真正用在溝通上的障礙。要考好英檢也許需要熟悉很多應試技巧，但這些技巧在真實情境裡是用不上的，當你聽不懂對方說什麼的時候，他們的臉上不會出現 A、B、C、D 四個選項讓你去選最可能的答案，你必須立即想出唯一正確的答案，否則你硬是無法回應人家的話，這也許就是我前述的那位多益八百多分的空姐遇到的情形。這也是這本書真正希望幫助讀者達到的目標：不只通過英檢測驗，還要通過真實溝通情境的考驗。

2. 群組法的障礙：

　　我們平常說話都是一句一句說，最少一次也會有兩個字以上的「字串」，像「你好」、「這樣」、那樣」、「出來講」……等等。所以我們還可以看見這些話在聊天室裡寫成「鳥」、「醬」、「釀」、「踹共」……等等。這是我們說話的天性，英語也是一樣的，所以我們常見 going to, want to, should have, got to 等等寫成 gonna, wanna, shoulda, gotta 等等。如果你聽人說話時腦中一直想著他所說的到底是哪些個別的字，那當然是聽不懂的。所以就必須習於這種常見連音的意思，這在坊間的各種英檢課本裡都有特別整理這些常聽到的連音字，特別是初級與中級的課本。

3. 贅語的障礙：

　　這項障礙就與英檢考試無關了，這是現實情境裡才會遭遇的情形。口語和書面文字不一樣，他有很多贅語現象。考試其實是書面語，即使是聽力測驗也是已經寫好了錄音稿的書面語，它不會有「我的意思是」"I mean"，「你知道嗎」"You know?"等等口頭禪這樣的贅語。其實這些贅語往往是你聽懂對方的線索。這些贅語當然在準備英檢考試中是無法練習的，最好的辦法是找真人練習，也就是我們課程中所設計給你與伙伴的自由對談中練習，若課程內容所不足的，或許可以一起找一部電影，一邊看一邊討論劇情（當然是用英語），但看電影的時候就注意，言談者所用的贅語與他們真正要說的意思之間的線索。

4. 簡化詞語：

　　這一點與群組法是相通的，除了把幾個字連成一個字 (I will = I'll; Did you eat yet? = Dijjtyet) 之外，還有句法的簡化如問 "When will you be back?" 而回答 "Tomorrow, maybe" 這在聽力測驗中也是常見的，若你一向都用完整句子回答，遇見這種句子就可能困擾。

5. 表達的變項：

　　除非事先準備好的講稿（英檢測驗就是），一般的口語都是充滿了遲疑、錯誤的開始 (false start)、停頓 (pause)、修正 (correction)。母語人士是從小就學習如何除掉這些雜草，但是這些很容易干擾第二語言學習者的聽解。這也不會在英檢考試裡出現，也是必須練習與真人對話或看電影時細心去聽懂的。

此外就是我們以為任何標註 KK 音標上的音就是正確的發音，但是母語人士發音時，重音節上，s 後的 [p] [t] [k] 會變音成 [b] [d] [g]。例如：stupid 中重音是 stu，所以變音成 [sdju]；輕音節 pid 也一起變音成 [bɪd]。然而母語老師精確的說法是，[p] 的確變音了，但不是變成 [b]，而是 [p] 這個無聲子音不出氣，發音聽起來類似 [b]，是介於 [b] 與 [p] 的音。Hospital / spi 變音 [sbɪ]，非常輕音的 [b]。而 hospital / mosquito 中的 [t] 則變音成彈音 [d]。這些變音對於從小認真學 KK 音標而不曾注意實際母語人士變音的學者，也是一種困擾。

由於音準的辨識有困擾，在測驗中也就常有與問題內容類似音的答案選項來干擾，如 research「研究」與 search「搜尋」的對象不同，當然意思也不同。而 aware「察覺」與 wear「穿戴」意思就差更遠了。Project 與 reject 也可以是近似音混淆。許多初、中級英檢的課本會特別整理這些容易混淆的子音或母音，這方面有困擾的學者是有必要多朗誦這些類似的音，以熟習其間的差異。

現實情境中，母語人士也會溜嘴說出不合文法的句子如 "We arrived in a little town that there was no hotel anywhere." 或是方言如 "I don't get no respect." 這些在考試中不會出現，卻常在電影中聽得到的句子，也可能是死讀書的學者要適應的。

6. 口語體：

　　如 "Fred's new novel has been selling like hot cakes" 這類的俗語，是平日要多多記誦的，有許多幾乎是字面意思無法理解的，如 "It rains cats and dogs"（大雨滂沱）；"He has a sweet tooth"（他愛吃甜食）；"he is under weather"（他不舒服）等等包括成語 (idioms)、俚語 (slang)、簡化語、特殊風俗民情等等，不論是獨白或對話都常出現，當然考試就少不了它們。由於不熟習俗語的學者會對字面上意義的誤解，在答案選項中就會有以字面解釋的選項來混淆，例如這句 Fred's new novel has been selling like hot cakes. 就可以拿 hot, cake, 甚至 cookies 來混淆：

A. Perhaps we should go on a cooler day.

B. So, how do you like the cake?

C. You mean he ate all of the cookies?

7. 說話速度：

　　有些人覺得外國人說話太快，其實研究者發現並不是因為講得快，而是說話者停頓的次數太少或連續說話的時間太長所致。這是我們在測驗中或是聽演講時才會遇見的情形，與真人溝通的時候，我們總可以打斷對方一下，讓他不要一直講下去，這也是有些人不敢與母語人士交談的原因，因為在平常應考的練習中從未有機會打斷對方，卻只有答錯的壓力，放在實際溝通的情境裡，這種壓力就如影隨形的威脅著你的互動能力，破壞了說話的互動本能，再加上自己對自己預期的表現太高，這種怕錯的心理壓力更強了，自然會逼著多益八百多分的人只能說咖啡與茶兩個字了。

8. 重音、節奏、與語調：

英語每個單字的音節數量不同，把一堆字放在句子裡必須以重音記次 (stress-timed) 來標示出聽見的各個單字，也就是一個句子裡每個字有一個重音，每個重音讓你聽出那是一個字。而中文每個字都是單音節，在標示單字的功能上與英文不同，這也是一些習慣一個字一個字聽與讀學習者的困擾。除了重音的差別，英語的一個特色是，同樣的兩個字，重音在前在後會形成完全不同的意思，例如下列字串的比較（大寫代表重音）：（打開音檔隨母語人士複誦）🎧 **Mp3 002**

Hotdog	熱狗	hot DOG	一隻很熱的狗
BAREback	無鞍的馬背	bare Back	裸背
BLACKberry	黑莓	black BERRY	黑色的莓子
BOLDface	粗體字	bold FACE	醒目的臉
ODDball	古怪的人	odd BALL	奇怪的球
GREENhouse	溫室	green HOUSE	綠色的房子
GREENbelt	綠色地帶	green BELT	綠色的腰帶
BLUEgress	早熟的禾屬植物	blue GRASS	藍色的草
HIGHtop	高於踝骨的	high TOP	高的山、屋頂
DARKroom	沖印暗房	dark ROOM	黑暗的房間
REDcoat*	英國陸軍	red COAT	紅色的外套

* 英國陸軍的別稱書寫體須是專有名詞 Red coat 或 Redcoat

DAY ② TUESDAY

做過多益題型，我們再體驗一回模擬的全民英檢聽力測驗，請大家打開音檔，一起做第一部份。

看圖辨義

本部份共 **15** 題，試題冊上有數幅圖畫，每一圖畫有 **1 ～ 3** 個描述該圖之題目，每題請聽錄音機播出題目以及 **A、B、C、D** 四個英語敘述之後，選出與所看到的圖畫最相符的答案，每題只播出一遍。

🎧 **Mp3 003**

A. Questions 1-2

B. Question 3

C. Question 4

D. Questions 5-7

E. Questions 8-9

F. Question 10

G. Questions 11-12

H. Question 13

I. Question 14

J. Question 15

核對答案：

1. B 2. C 3. B 4. B 5. A 6. D 7. D 8. A 9. C 10. C

11. B 12. A 13. B 14. D 15. C

接下來再播放 **1-15** 題一遍，隨著音軌的播放，找同伴練習問答，練習時甲同學按下列問題內容問乙同學，乙同學回答正確答案。注意！盡量模仿母語人士的口音、音調以及不同情境所表現的情感，乙同學此時已經知道該選的答案，所以要特別注意聽要回答的選項。

播放：**For questions number 1 and 2, please look at picture A.**
Question number 1: What does the picture show? 暫停

甲複誦： Question number 1: What does the picture show? 繼續撥放四個答案

乙回答： (B) They're looking at a view.

播放：**Question number 2:** Which description matches the picture? 暫停

甲複誦： Question number 2: Which description matches the picture? 繼續撥放四個答案

乙回答： (A) The girl has long hair.

預判出現的字彙有：water, lake, looking at, scenery, view, short hair, hat 等。

播放：**For question number 3, please look at picture B.**

Question number 3: A bakery is preparing Dorayaki. Which of the following information is true? 暫停

> 甲複誦： Question number 3: A bakery is preparing Dorayaki. Which of the following information is true? 繼續撥放四個答案
>
> 乙回答： (B) The red beans are filled inside the Dorayaki.

> 預判出現的字彙有：Dorayaki, box, cup, table 等。

播放：**For question number 4, please look at picture C.**

Question number 4: Which description matches the picture? 暫停

> 甲複誦： Question number 4: Which description matches the picture? 繼續撥放四個答案
>
> 乙回答： (B) The girl is in front of the statue.

> 預判出現的字彙有：statue, Buddha, girl, worship, in front of, near, next to 等。

播放：**For questions number 5 to 7, please look at picture D.**

Question number 5: Look at Joanna. What's she holding? 暫停

> 甲複誦： Question number 5: Look at Joanna. What's she holding? 繼續撥放四個答案
>
> 乙回答： (A) She's holding a scoop.

> 預判出現的字彙有：scoop, shovel, dig, plant, dirt, soil, raincoat 等。

播音內容

1: What does the picture show?

　　(A) It's hot and rainy today.

　　(B) They're looking at a view.

　　(C) They're washing a suit.

　　(D) There are a lot of swimmers in the water.

1：圖片說明了什麼？

　　(A) 今天又熱又多雨。

　　(B) 他們在看一個景色。

　　(C) 她們洗一套西裝。

　　(D) 有很多的游泳運動員在水中。

2: Which description matches the picture?

　　(A) They all have short hair.

　　(B) They are wearing hats.

　　(C) The girl has long hair.

　　(D) The boy is wearing short pants.

2：哪種描述與照片相符？

　　(A) 他們都有短的頭髮。

　　(B) 他們都戴著帽子。

　　(C) 這個女孩有長頭髮。

　　(D) 男孩穿著短的褲子。

3: A bakery is preparing Dorayaki. Which of the following information is true?

(A) The cup is in front of the table.

(B) The red beans are filled inside the Dorayaki.

(C) A wallet with flowers is on the front.

(D) There are flowers inside the cup.

3：一家麵包店正在準備銅鑼燒蛋糕。其中以下資訊是真的？

(A) 杯子放在桌子前方。

(B) 紅豆填充在銅鑼燒蛋糕裡面。

(C) 綴著鮮花的錢包放在前面。

(D) 杯子裡面有花。

4: Which description matches the picture?

(A) The statue is next to the girl.

(B) The girl is in front of the statue.

(C) The TV is across from the statue.

(D) The TV is next to the girl.

4：哪種描述與照片相符？

(A) 這尊雕像是在女孩的身旁。

(B) 女孩在雕像前。

(C) 電視在這座雕像對面。

(D) 電視在女孩的身旁。

5: Look at Joanna. What's she holding?

(A) She's holding a scoop.

(B) She's holding a raincoat.

(C) She's holding a hood.

(D) She's holding a pack.

5：看看瓊安娜。她拿著什麼？

(A) 她拿著一把鏟子。

(B) 她拿著一件雨衣。

(C) 她握著頭套。

(D) 她握著一個包袱。

播放：**Question number 6:** Look at Joanna again. What is she doing? 暫停

甲複誦： Question number 6: Look at Joanna again. What is she doing? 繼續撥放四個答案

乙回答： (D) She's digging the soil.

> 預判出現的字彙有：scoop, shovel, dig, plant, dirt, soil, raincoat 等。

播放：**Question number 7:** Look at the two persons behind Joanna. What are they wearing? 暫停

甲複誦： Question number 7: Look at the two persons behind Joanna. What are they wearing? 繼續撥放四個答案

乙回答： (D) They are wearing raincoats.

> 預判出現的字彙有：shovel, dig, plant, dirt, soil, raincoat 等。

播放：For questions number 8 and 9, please look at picture E.
Question number 8: A boy is in a classroom. What are in front of him? 暫停

    甲複誦： Question number 8: A boy is in a classroom. What are in front of him? 繼續撥放四個答案

    乙回答： (A) Two buckets of water.

> 預判出現的字彙有：
> sign, buckets, poster, classroom, workshop 等。

播放：Question number 9: What does the classroom look like? 暫停

    甲複誦： Question number 9: What does the classroom look like? 繼續撥放四個答案

    乙回答： (C) On the front, you can see a black poster with signs.

> 預判出現的字彙有：sign, buckets, poster, classroom, workshop 等。

播放：For question number 10, please look at picture F.
Question number 10: How are the wooden zebras located? 暫停

    甲複誦： Question number 10: How are the wooden zebras located? 繼續撥放四個答案

    乙回答： (C) One of them is in front of the billboard.

> 預判出現的字彙有：
> wooden zebra, billboard, trash can, beverage vending machines, car, scooters 等。

6: Look at Joanna again. What is she doing?

(A) She's cutting the plant.

(B) She's sweeping the floor.

(C) She's piling up some dirt.

(D) She's digging the soil.

6：再看看瓊安娜。她正在做什麼？

(A) 她正在切割植物。

(B) 她正在掃地。

(C) 她堆積一些泥土。

(D) 她正在挖土。

7: Look at the two persons behind Joanna. What are they wearing?

(A) They are wearing shorts.

(B) They are wearing skirts.

(C) They are wearing gloves.

(D) They are wearing raincoats.

7：看看瓊安娜背後的兩人。他們穿的是什麼？

(A) 他們穿著短褲。

(B) 他們穿著裙子。

(C) 他們都戴著手套。

(D) 他們穿著雨衣。

8: A boy is in a classroom. What are in front of him?

   (A) Two buckets of water.

   (B) Two bucks on a counter.

   (C) Tools on the table.

   (D) Two washing machines.

8：一個男孩在教室裡。在他面前的是什麼？

   (A) 兩桶水。

   (B) 在櫃檯上的兩塊錢。

   (C) 在桌子上的工具。

   (B) 兩個洗衣機。

9: What does the classroom look like?

   (A) There're no signs in the front of the classroom.

   (B) There's a teacher in the front of classroom.

   (C) On the front, you can see a black poster with signs.

   (D) There're no posters on the wall.

9：教室像什麼樣子？

   (A) 教室前面沒有標誌。

   (B) 教室前面有一位老師在。

   (C) 你可以看到一個黑色海報與標誌在前面。

   (D) 牆上沒有海報。

10: How are the wooden zebras located?

(A) They're behind the beverage vending machines.

(B) They're in front of the scooters.

(C) One of them is in front of the billboard.

(D) One of them is next to the billboard.

10. 木製斑馬位於何處？

(A) 他們在飲料自動販賣機後面。

(B) 他們在機車前面。

(C) 其中之一在看板前面。

(D) 其中之一在看板旁邊

播放：For questions number 11 and 12, please look at picture G.

Question number 11: What do the cages show? 暫停

甲複誦： Question number 11: What do the cages show? 繼續
撥放四個答案

乙回答： (B) The dog is in a vest.

播放：Question number 12: Look at the cages again. Where is the dog looking at? 暫停

甲複誦： Question number 12: Look at the cages again. Where is the dog looking at? 繼續撥放四個答案

乙回答： (A) He is looking at his left.

預判出現的字彙有：cage, dog, vest, wooden, steel, left, looking at, behind the bars 等。

播放：For question number 13, please look at picture H.

Question number 13: What are they probably doing? 暫停

    甲複誦： Question number 13: What are they probably doing?

        繼續撥放四個答案

    乙回答： (B) Waiting to check in far from the counter.

> 預判出現的字彙有：
>
> airport, man, boy, cold, coat, shirt, waiting line, counter, checking in 等。

播放：For question number 14, please look at picture I.

Question number 14: What's the traffic situation on the highway? 暫停

    甲複誦： Question number 14: What's the traffic situation on the highway? **繼續撥放四個答案**

    乙回答： (D) There's been an accident. A car has just hit the rail.

> 預判出現的字彙有：traffic, accident, car, rail, driver, traffic jam 等。

播放：For question number 15, please look at picture J.

Question number 15: Which instructions match the pictures? 暫停

    甲複誦： Question number 15: Which instructions match the pictures? **繼續撥放四個答案**

    乙回答： (C) The train is arriving. Please get ready to board.

> 預判出現的字彙有：train, station, platform, board, alight, arriving 等。

播音內容

11: What do the cages show?

(A) There're two dogs in the cages.

(B) The dog is in a vest.

(C) The cages are all made of wood.

(D) The cages are all made of steel.

11：籠子裡展示了什麼？

(A) 有兩條狗在籠子裡。

(B) 這條狗穿了一件背心。

(C) 籠子裡都是木製的。

(D) 籠子裡都是鋼製的。

12: Where is the dog looking?

(A) He is looking at his left.

(B) He is looking at his right.

(C) He is looking forward.

(D) He is looking behind.

12：這狗看哪裡？

(A) 牠看著牠的左邊。

(B) 牠看著牠的右邊。

(C) 牠看著前方。

(D) 牠看著後面。

13: What are they probably doing?

(A) Talking with the lady behind them.

(B) Waiting to check in far from the counter.

(C) Waiting to check in near the counter.

(D) Shopping in the convenience store.

13：他們大概在做什麼？

(A) 跟他們後面的女士交談。

(B) 在櫃檯遠處等待辦理登機手續。

(C) 在櫃檯附近等待辦理登機手續。

(D) 在便利店裡購物。

14: What's the traffic situation on the highway?

(A) A car was hit by a truck, so traffic is moving very slowly.

(B) The highway is closed for road maintenance.

(C) Traffic is moving quite smoothly at this time of the day.

(D) There's been an accident. A car has just hit the rail.

14：在高速公路上的交通狀況如何？

(A) 車被一輛卡車撞了，所以交通很緩慢。

(B) 道路因維修封閉。

(C) 車流此時移動得很順利。

(D) 出事了，一輛車剛撞上了護欄。

15: Which instruction matches the pictures?

(A) The train has arrived. All passengers please alight.

(B) The doors are about to close. Please keep clear of the doors.

(C) <u>The train is arriving. Please get ready to board.</u>

(D) Here we are at the terminal station. Thank you for your patronage.

15：哪一指令符合圖片？

(A) 火車已經到了。所有的乘客請下車。

(B) 門即將關閉。請保持門口淨空。

(C) 列車即將進站。請準備好上車。

(D) 我們到終點站了。謝謝您的惠顧。

DAY 3 WEDNESDAY

上一回是模擬的英檢聽力測驗，這一回我們再體驗一次模擬的多益聽力測驗，現在請大家打開音檔，一起做多益第一部份「圖片描述」。

Picture Description

Look and choose the statement that best describes what you see in the picture. Mp3 004

1.

2.

3.

4.

5.

6.

7.

8.

9.

10.

核對答案：

1. B　2. B　3. A　4. B　5. C　6. C　7. D　8. A　9. C　10. A

接下來再播放 **1-10** 題一遍，隨著音軌的播放，找同伴練習問答，練習時甲同學按下列問題內容問乙同學，乙同學回答正確答案。注意！盡量模仿母語人士的口音、音調以及不同情境所表現的情感，乙同學此時已經知道該選的答案，所以要特別注意聽要回答的選項。

甲個別播放 ABCD 四選項，每播完一項暫停，再複誦：

1. (A) They are jogging on the tracks.

   (B) They are walking on the tracks.

   (C) The woman is waking in the field.

   (D) The weather is cloudy.

   乙回答：(B) They are walking on the tracks.

   > 預判出現的字彙為：tracks, students, teacher, field, walking, running 等。

甲個別播放 ABCD 四選項，每播完一項暫停，再複誦：

2. (A) The bird on the top is walking.

   (B) The bird on the floor is walking.

   (C) The bird on the top is dancing.

   (D) Bird on the floor is singing.

   乙回答：(B) The bird on the floor is walking.

   > 預判出現的字彙為：birds, on the top, on the floor, walking 等。

甲個別播放 **ABCD** 四選項，每播完一項暫停，再複誦：

3. (A) The man is sitting in the horse-drawn carriage.

   (B) The horse is running away.

   (C) The man is sitting in the front of the carriage.

   (D) They are having a picnic in a park.

   乙回答：(A) The man is sitting in the horse-drawn carriage.

   > 預判出現的字彙為：
   > horse-drawn carriage, coachman, street, park, in the back of, in the front of 等。

甲個別播放 **ABCD** 四選項，每播完一項暫停，再複誦：

4. (A) The woman is sleeping in the room.

   (B) The woman is weaving by the loom.

   (C) The woman is sweeping the broom.

   (D) The woman is sitting on the broom.

   乙回答：(B) The woman is weaving by the loom.

   > 預判出現的字彙為：woman, loom, weaving, 等。

甲個別播放 **ABCD** 四選項，每播完一項暫停，再複誦：

5. (A) The men are sitting at the table.

   (B) The ash tray is on the floor.

   (C) The table is behind them.

   (D) The man is talking to the woman.

   乙回答：(C) The table is behind them.

   > 預判出現的字彙為：
   > men, woman, mountain, scenery, table, trash can, in row 等。

播音內容

1. (A) They are jogging on the tracks.

   (B) They are walking on the tracks.

   (C) The woman is walking in the field.

   (D) The weather is cloudy.

解析：	(A) 他們都在跑道上慢跑。
(A) (C) 是對運動場上場地名稱的認知，以及人物動作的認知考驗，(D) 是環境觀察考驗。	(B) 他們正在跑道上走著。
	(C) 女人在田賽場中走著。
	(D) 天氣是多雲的。

2. (A) The bird on the top is walking.

   (B) The bird on the floor is walking.

   (C) The bird on the top is dancing.

   (D) Bird on the floor is singing.

解析：	(A) 在上面的鳥走著。
(A) (C) (D) 是對動物動作的認知考驗。	(B) 在地板上的鳥走著。
	(C) 在上面的鳥跳著舞。
	(D) 在地板上的小鳥在唱歌。

3. (A) The man is sitting in the horse-drawn carriage.

   (B) The horse is running away.

   (C) The man is sitting in the front of the carriage.

   (D) They are having a picnic in a park.

解析：	(A) 這個人坐在馬車裡。
(B) 是對動物動作的認知考驗。	(B) 馬跑開了。
(C) 是對人物位置的認知考驗。	(C) 那個男人坐在馬車的前面。
(D) 是對人物動作的認知考驗。	(D) 他們在公園裡野餐。

4. (A) The woman is sleeping in the room.
   (B) The woman is weaving by the loom.
   (C) The woman is sweeping the broom.
   (D) The woman is sitting on the broom.

解析：	(A) 女人在房間裡睡覺。
(A) (B) (D) 是對人物動作的認知考驗，(D) 另對人物位置也誤導，而且本題特別在發音上的類同 "room, loom"、"weaving, sleeping, sitting" 也設計了考驗。	(B) 女人用機杼織布。
	(C) 女人正在揮掃。
	(D) 這個女人正坐在掃帚上。

5. A. The men are sitting at the table.
   B. The ash tray is on the floor.
   C. The table is behind them.
   D. The man is talking to the woman.

解析：	(A) 男子正坐在桌旁。
(A) (B) 對人物位置誤導，(D) 對人物動作的認知考驗。	(B) 煙灰盤在地板上。
	(C) 桌子在他們身後。
	(D) 男人和女人說話

甲個別播放 ABCD 四選項，每播完一項暫停，再複誦：

6. (A) There is a price sign beside the stand.

   (B) The stand is full of vegetables.

   (C) The stand is full of fruits.

   (D) The price is two thousand and two hundred.

   乙回答：(C) The stand is full of fruits.

   > 預判出現的字彙為：price sign, fruits, vegetables, stands, packs 等。

甲個別播放 ABCD 四選項，每播完一項暫停，再複誦：

7. (A) The sky is clear.

   (B) There is only one boat on the sea.

   (C) The boats are full of fish.

   (D) The weather is cloudy.

   乙回答：The weather is cloudy.

   > 預判出現的字彙為：boat, sea, ocean, sky, sailing, weather 等。

甲個別播放 ABCD 四選項，每播完一項暫停，再複誦：

8. (A) The woman is waiting by the stand.

   (B) The woman is buying something.

   (C) The stand is full of books.

   (D) The woman is cleaning the table.

   乙回答：The woman is waiting by the stand.

   > 預判出現的字彙為：price, stands, packs, waiting, serving, selling 等。

甲個別播放 ABCD 四選項，每播完一項暫停，再複誦：

9. (A) The tree stands in the path.

   (B) The path is crowded with people.

   (C) The path is paved across the lawn.

   (D) The path is surrounded by water.

   乙回答：The path is paved across the lawn.

> 預判出現的字彙為：trail, path, pave, lawn, palm trees, water, reeds 等。

甲個別播放 ABCD 四選項，每播完一項暫停，再複誦：

10. (A) The horse is probably waiting for his passenger.

   (B) The horse is walking on the street.

   (C) The horse is ridden by a man.

   (D) The horse is eating by the road.

   乙回答：The horse is probably waiting for his passenger.

> 預判出現的字彙為：horse, waiting, serving, hat, mask 等。

【Day 3】Wednesday

播音內容

6. (A) There is a price sign beside the stand.

(B) The stand is full of vegetables.

(C) The stand is full of fruits.

(D) The price is two thousand and two hundred.

解析：	(A) 價格標誌立在攤子旁邊。
(A) 誤導位置。	(B) 攤子放滿了蔬菜。
(B) 考驗景物存在。	(C) 攤子放滿了水果。
(D) 考驗數字認知。	(D) 價格是二千兩百。

7. (A) The sky is clear.

(B) There is only one boat on the sea.

(C) The boats are full of fish.

(D) The weather is cloudy.

解析：	(A) 天空是明朗的。
(A) 誤導環境認知。	(B) 海上只有一艘船。
(B) 考驗景物存在。	(C) 小船都裝滿了魚。
(C) 考驗景物存在。	(D) 天氣是多雲的。

8. (A) The woman is waiting by the stand.

(B) The woman is buying something.

(C) The stand is full of books.

(D) The woman is cleaning the table.

解析：	(A) 女人在攤子旁服務。
(B) (D) 誤導人物動作認知。	(B) 女人在買東西。
(C) 考驗景物存在。	(C) 攤子上全是書。
	(D) 女人正在收拾餐桌。

9. (A) The tree stands in the path.

(B) The path is crowded with people.

(C) The path is paved across the lawn.

(D) The path is surrounded by water.

解析：	(A) 這棵樹立在小徑中央。
(A) 誤導位置認知。	(B) 小徑擠滿了人。
(B) 考驗景物存在。	(C) 小徑是穿過草坪鋪成的。
(D) 考驗空間安排。	(D) 小徑四面環水。

10. (A) The horse is probably waiting for his passenger.

(B) The horse is walking on the street.

(C) The horse is ridden by a man.

(D) The horse is eating by the road.

解析：	(A) 這匹馬可能在等牠的乘客。
(B) (D) 誤導動物動作認知。	(B) 這匹馬在街上走著。
(C) 考驗景物存在。	(C) 一個人騎著這匹馬。
	(D) 這匹馬在路邊吃東西。

DAY 4 THURSDAY

　　第一節（Day1）我們以聽力測驗的題型分析更進一步理解了看圖口說的技巧。從題型中我們瞭解一般圖示的動詞時態多為現在簡單式與現在進行式，這一節我們要針對現在進行式與動名詞的混淆語意做一番釐清。這是一般人很少注意的混淆情形，但是在真正與母語人士溝通時卻是很容易誤會的。因此這一節我們一開始先隨著母語人士練習一下同樣的兩個字，重音在前在後的不同發音，體會其完全不同的意思，除了重音在前在後會形成完全不同的意思之外，其文法的含意也不同（畫底線代表重音）：

請播音檔，每句暫停，複誦： Mp3 005

They're **dry**ing cloths.（那些是用來擦乾的布。）
They're drying **cloths**.（他們正在把布弄乾。）

They're **hik**ing trails.（那些是步道。）
They're hiking **trails**.（他們正在步道上散步。）

They're **plan**ning meetings.（那些是為計畫而開的會議。）
They're planning **meetings**.（他們正在計畫開會。）

They're **rac**ing bikes.（那些是比賽用自行車。）
They're racing **bikes**.（他們正在比賽自行車。）

They're **sail**ing ships.（那些是大帆船。）

They're sailing **ships**.（他們正在揚帆行駛。）

They're **advertis**ing companies.（那些是廣告公司。）

They're advertising **companies**.（他們正在做公司的廣告。）

They're **mail**ing envelopes.（那些是郵寄用的信封。）

They're mailing **envelopes**.（他們正在寄送信封。）

They're **cut**ting boards.（那些是砧板。）

They're cutting **boards**.（那些機器正在切割木板。）

【Day 4】
Thursday

這十組完全一樣的句子，之所以意思不一樣在於前一句都是動名詞與名詞的組合字，後一句則是現在進行動詞的分詞與受詞。而唸出來的讀音就必須按上述的重音的讀法，才能區分二者的意思。由於動名詞與分詞一樣，都是在原型動詞字尾加上 ing，但意義卻完全不同，我們先就現在分詞舉例說明，在舉出動名詞的不同用法以比較。

接著我們再如上一節一樣，再練習十題聽解與複誦然後理解題型分析以加強口說基礎。

Picture Description

Look and choose the statement that best describes what you see in the picture. Mp3 006

1.

2.   3.

4.

5.

6.

7.

8.

9.

10.

【Day 4】
Thursday

核對答案：

1. D　2. B　3. B　4. C　5. B　6. A　7. B　8. D　9. B　10. C

接下來再播放 **1-10** 題一遍，隨著音軌的播放，找同伴練習問答，練習時甲同學按下列問題內容問乙同學，乙同學回答正確答案。注意！盡量模仿母語人士的口音、音調以及不同情境所表現的情感，乙同學此時已經知道該選的答案，所以要特別注意聽要回答的選項。

甲個別播放每題 ABCD 四選項，每播完一項暫停，再複誦：

1. Look at picture No. 1.

    (A) The boy is smiling.

    (B) The boy is wearing a cap.

    (C) The girl is crying.

    (D) The girl is wearing a hat.

    乙回答：(D) The girl is wearing a hat.

預判出現的字彙有：smiling, crying, hat 等。

2. Look at picture No. 2.

    (A) People are in a flea market.

    (B) People are in an arcade.

    (C) People are in a department store.

    (D) There is no crowd in this picture.

    乙回答：(B) People are in an arcade.

預判出現的字彙有：arcade（騎樓）, T-shirt, shorts, sneakers 等。

3. Look at picture No. 3.

(A) A girl is washing a pan.

(B) A girl is cooking with pan.

(C) A girl is turning the pan.

(D) A girl is searching for the pan.

乙回答：(B) A girl is cooking with pan.

預判出現的字彙有：pan, cooking, apron, T-shirt stirring 等。

4. Look at picture No. 4.

(A) The path is crowded.

(B) There are two statues in the caves.

(C) The caves are behind the waterfall.

(D) The girls are chatting in front of a fountain.

乙回答：(C) The caves are behind the waterfall.

預判出現的字彙有：waterfall, caves, path, trail, track, rail, cliff 等。

【Day 4】
Thursday

5. Look at picture No. 5.

(A) The trees are real plants.

(B) The trees are bound with barrier tapes.

(C) The trees are surrounded with people.

(D) The trees are blocked by police.

乙回答：(B) The trees are bound with barrier tapes.

預判出現的字彙有：trees, tapes, sign, bind(bound), blocked, surrounded 等。

播音內容

Look at picture No. 1.

    (A) The boy is smiling.

    (B) The boy is wearing a cap.

    (C) The girl is crying.

    (D) The girl is wearing a hat.

解析：	(A) 那個男孩笑了。
(A)(C) 考驗面部表情的認知。	(B) 那個男孩戴著一頂棒球帽。
(B) 考驗外貌特徵的認知。	(C) 那個女孩正在哭。
	(D) 那個女孩戴著一頂帽子。

Look at picture No. 2.

    (A) People are in a flea market.

    (B) People are in an arcade.

    (C) People are in a department store.

    (D) There is no crowd in this picture.

解析：	(A) 人們在跳蚤市場。
(A)(C) 誤導位置、環境的認知，	(B) 人們在騎樓裡。
(D) 考驗景物存在的認知。	(C) 人們在一家百貨公司內。
	(D) 在這幅畫中沒有人群。

Look at picture No. 3.

    (A) A girl is washing a pan.

    (B) A girl is cooking with pan.

    (C) A girl is turning the pan.

    (D) A girl is searching for the pan.

解析：	(A) 女孩洗盤子。
(A) (C) (D) 考驗對人物動作的認知。	(B) 女孩正在用平底鍋烹製。
	(C) 女孩攪動平底鍋。
	(D) 女孩正在尋找平底鍋。

Look at picture No. 4.

   (A) The path is crowded.

   (B) There are two statues in the caves.

   (C) The caves are behind the waterfall.

   (D) The girls are chatting in front of a fountain.

解析：	(A) 路徑是擁擠的。
(A) (B) (D) 考驗景物存在的認知。	(B) 有兩個雕像在洞穴裡。
	(C) 洞穴在瀑布的後面。
	(D) 少女們在噴泉前聊天。

【Day 4】Thursday

Look at picture No. 5.

   (A) The trees are real plants.

   (B) The trees are bound with barrier tapes.

   (C) The trees are surrounded with people.

   (D) The trees are blocked by police.

解析：	(A) 樹是真正的植物。
(A) 考驗材質的認知，(C) (D) 考驗景物存在的認知。	(B) 樹木被隔離帶纏繞。
	(C) 樹木周圍著人。
	(D) 樹被警方封鎖了。

甲個別播放每題 ABCD 四選項，每播完一項暫停，再複誦：

6.Look at picture No. 6.

　(A) The swings are behind the tree.

　(B) The path is behind the tree.

　(C) Two boys are playing on the swings.

　(D) The ladders are close to the tree.

　乙回答：(A) The swings are behind the tree.

預判會出現字彙有：swings, trail, path, track, tree, ladders 等。

7. Look at picture No. 7.

　(A) The stilt walker is kicking the crowds.

　(B) The stilt walker is holding an umbrella.

　(C) The woman is helping him up.

　(D) All of the crowds are walking stilts.

　乙回答：(B) The stilt walker is holding an umbrella.

預判會出現字彙有：stilt walker, umbrella, bra, hat, feather, skirt, pants, audience, crowd 等。

8. Look at picture No. 8.

　(A) The statue is wearing a jacket.

　(B) The statue is holding a bat.

　(C) They are working on the street.

　(D) They are lifting a statue on their shoulders.

　乙回答：(D) They are lifting a statue on their shoulders.

預判會出現字彙有：statue, Super Mario, men in diapers, lifting 等。

9.Look at picture No. 9.

(A) The woman is ready to jump.

(B) The woman is waving her hand.

(C) The woman is chatting with the others.

(D) The woman is lying on the float.

預判會出現字彙有：woman, float, ROC flags, waving 等。

乙回答：(B) The woman is waving her hand.

10. Look at picture No.10.

(A) Some people are playing behind basketball stands.

(B) The court is full of basketballs.

(C) A man is standing by the basketball stands.

(D) They are standing at the main gate.

乙回答：(C) A man is standing by the basketball stands.

預判會出現字彙有：basketball stands, basketball court, students, sports jacket 等。

【Day 4】
Thursday

播音內容

6. Look at picture No. 6.

(A) The swings are behind the tree.

(B) The path is behind the tree.

(C) Two boys are playing the swings.

(D) The ladders are close to the tree.

解析：	(A) 鞦韆在樹的後面。
(B) (D) 誤導位置、環境、空間	(B) 路徑在樹的後面。
安排，(C) 考驗景物存在的認	(C) 兩個男孩正在玩鞦韆。
知。	(D) 梯子貼近樹。

7. Look at picture No. 7.

(A) The stilt walker is kicking the crowds.

(B) The stilt walker is holding an umbrella.

(C) The woman is helping him up.

(D) All of the crowds are walking stilts.

解析：	(A) 高蹺人踢群眾。
(A) (C) (D) 考驗人物動作的認	(B) 高蹺人拿著一把傘。
知。	(C) 這個女人幫他的忙。
	(D) 所有的人都走高蹺。

8. Look at picture No. 8.

(A) The statue is wearing a jacket.

(B) The statue is holding a bat.

(C) They are walking on the street.

(D) They are lifting a statue on their shoulders.

| 解析：
(A) (B) 考驗外貌特徵的認知，
(C) 考驗人物動作的認知。 | (A) 這座雕像穿件夾克。
(B) 這座雕像拿著一支棒子。
(C) 他們正走在大街上。
(D) 他們把雕像舉在他們的肩膀上。 |

9. Look at picture No. 9.

(A) The woman is ready to jump.

(B) The woman is waving her hand.

(C) The woman is chatting with the others.

(D) The woman is lying on the float.

| 解析：
(A) (B) (D) 考驗人物動作的認知。 | (A) 這個女人準備要跳。
(B) 這個女人揮舞著她的手。
(C) 這個女人在與他人聊天。
(D) 這個女人正躺在花車上。 |

10. Look at picture No.10.

(A) Some people are playing behind basketball stands.

(B) The court is full of basketballs.

(C) A man is standing by the basketball stands.

(D) They are standing at the main gate.

| 解析：
(A) 考驗景物存在及動作的認知，(B) (D) 考驗景物存在的認知。 | (A) 有些人在打籃球架背後打球。
(B) 球場滿是籃球。
(C) 一個男人正站籃球架旁。
(D) 他們站在大門口。 |

最後這一節我們把圖片描述的測驗要領整理成幾個重點，以這幾個重點做題型分析，練習十題聽解然後複誦加強口說基礎。

1. 位置

這種題型通常針對人與物與其他人與物位置的關係，因此有關於位置的介系詞就是我們要特別注意聽與描述的。如：（請開音檔隨聲複誦） Mp3 007

above, against, among, at, at the back of, at the end of, atop, before, behind, below, beneath, between, by, close to, in, inside, in front of, near, next to, on, on top of, over, under 等等。

2. 動作

第一節我們在檢討中提過動作多半是現在進行式與現在式，所以要注意同樣是動詞原型 VR+ing 的形式，卻有現在分詞與動名詞的運用的不同，這裡我們要再補充除了現在分詞所表現的主動語態 (be+V-ing)，還有過去分詞所表現的被動語態 (be+V-ed)，因此要注意常見的主動語被動分詞：（請開音檔隨聲複誦） Mp3 008

A. 主動

cleaning, crossing, cutting, drawing, drinking, eating, holding, jogging, listening, loading, locking, making, packing, playing, pouring, pulling, pushing, selling, setting, sitting, speaking, stretching, sweeping, talking, typing, walking, watching, watering, working, wrapping, writing...

B. 被動

being + cleaned, cleared, displayed, dug up, handed, locked, painted, planted, poled, pilled, served, set up, towed, walked, washed, watered, wrapped...

3. 情態

這類題目問的是圖中事物的情況或狀態，所以要注意的是圖中的焦點並想向你自己將如何描述這個情境，通常就要用到下列的形容詞與過去分詞當形容詞的字：（請開音檔隨聲複誦） 🎧 Mp3 009

A. 形容詞

afraid, asleep, beautiful, bent, bright, clean, dark, dirty, empty, flat, full, happy, heavy, high, light, long, open, rainy, round, tall, sad, straight, wet...

B. 過去分詞當形容詞

arranged, blocked, broken, chained, cleared, closed, crowded, crushed, deserted, displayed, equipped, loaded, occupied, parked, piled, posted, scattered, seated, stacked, stranded, tried...

4. 同音混淆

在錯誤的選項中用同音字來混淆正確答案，常見類同字如下：

A. 母音近似的字（請開音檔隨聲複誦） 🎧 Mp3 010

afford / offer, awful / oval, ball / bawl, bike / hike, cheer / chair, clean / lean, coach / couch / , hitting / fitting, just /

adjust, lake / rake, lamp / ramp, law / raw, lean / learn, light / right, lock / rock, low / row, owl / foul, mail / rail, meal / wheal, on the / under, peach / speech, peel / pill, pine / fine, player / prayer, playing / plane, pool / pull, poor / four, possible / impossible, rag / bag, selling / sailing, sheer / share, shopping / chopping, talk / take, there / they're, try / tie, wait / weigh, walk / work, west / rest, wheel / will...

B. 相同的字根、自首、字尾

aboard / abroad / board, inboard / onboard, agree / disagree, appear / disappear, aware / unaware, close / enclose, extract / exhale, just / adjust, relay / delay, reread / relayed, rest / arrest, similar / dissimilar, terrible / terrific, tie / untie, tire / retire, type / retype, underworked / underused, undrinkable / unthinkable...

　　上述四個重點，固然是聽力測驗的要領，卻也是以後看圖敘述的重點。口說描述對於圖片中位置、動作、情境的要領是一樣的。而同音混淆的問題也一樣會在口說描述中是一項考驗，如果發音不清楚，就造成評分老師們的混淆了。所以口說測驗一開始就有朗讀測驗，這種容易混淆的發音可就不能大意了。

　　除了上述題型的分析之外，我們還可以再用同字不同重音，而顯示不同意義的字彙與圖示來做聽力練習與口說練習。

Picture Description

Look and choose the statement that best describes what you see in the picture.  Mp3 011

1. BAREback 無鞍的馬背

2. bare Back 裸背

3. BOLDface 粗體字

When using the bold weight within running text, **like this, and this,** there's really no need to use **bold punctuation** too!

4. bold FACE 醒目的臉

5. GREENhouse 溫室

6. green HOUSE 綠色的房子

7. GREEN belt 綠色地帶

8. green BELT 綠色的腰帶

9. HIGH top 高於踝骨的

10. high TOP 高的山、屋頂

核對答案：

1. A 2. C 3. B 4. B 5. C 6. B 7. B 8. A 9. B 10. B

11. C 12. A

接下來再播放 **1-10** 題一遍,隨著音軌的播放,找同伴練習問答,練習時甲同學按下列問題內容問乙同學,乙同學回答正確答案。注意!盡量模仿母語人士的口音、音調以及不同情境所表現的情感,乙同學此時已經知道該選的答案,所以要特別注意聽要回答的選項。

甲個別播放 ABCD 四選項,每播完一項暫停,再複誦:

1. (A) The woman is on the BAREback.

   (B) The horse is running with bare feet.

   (C) The woman is running the horse.

   (D) The woman is riding with bare BACK.

   乙回答:(A) The woman is on the BAREback.

   > 這是情態題,該注意的情態為:woman, horse, bareback 等。

2. (A) Everyone on the street is walking with bare BACK.

   (B) The man is riding a motorcycle.

   (C) The bare BACK man is walking.

   (D) All of the motorcycles have BARE backs.

   乙回答:(C) The bare BACK man is walking.

   > 這是情態題,該注意的情態為:man, motorcycle, bareback, walking 等。

【Day 5】Friday

播音內容

1. What does the picture show?

   (A) The woman is on the BAREback.

   (B) The horse is running with bare feet.

   (C) The woman is running the horse.

   (D) The woman is riding with bare BACK.

1. 圖片說明了什麼？

   (A) 那女人在無鞍馬背上。

   (B) 這匹馬赤腳跑步。

   (C) 那女人騎著那匹馬跑。

   (D) 那女人光著背騎馬。

2. Which description matches the picture?

   (A) Everyone on the street is walking with bare BACK.

   (B) The man is riding a motorcycle.

   (C) The bare BACK man is walking.

   (D) All of the motorcycles have BARE backs.

2. 哪種描述與圖片相符？

   (A) 每個人都裸露著背在街上走。

   (B) 那個人騎著一輛摩托車。

   (C) 裸背的人走著。

   (D) 所有的摩托車都沒座椅。

甲個別播放每題 ABCD 四選項，每播完一項暫停，再複誦：

3. Which of the following answers best describe the picture?

   (A) The passage is written in French.

   (B) The passage is written in bold FACE.

   (C) "Like this, and this" are written in BOLDface.

   (D) The passage is written by a man with bold FACE.

   乙回答：(C) "Like this, and this" are written in BOLDface.

> 這是情態題，該注意的情態為：passage, boldface 等。

4. Which of the following answers best describe the picture?

   (A) It's a bold FACE of woman.

   (B) It's a bold FACE of man.

   (C) The bold FACE has long hair.

   (D) The bold FACE wears long beard.

   乙回答：(C) It's a bold FACE of man.

> 這是情態題，該注意的情態為：man, boldface, moustache, glasses 等。

【Day 5】
Friday

5. Which of the following answers best describe the picture?

   (A) The plants are all in the GREENhouse.

   (B) There is no one in the GREENhouse.

   (C) The GREENhouse is full of plants.

   (D) There are a lot of flowers in the greenHOUSE.

   乙回答：(B) There is no one in the GREENhouse.

> 這是情態題，該注意的情態為：greenhouse, plants 等。

6. Which of the following answers best describe the picture?

(A) The plants are all in the GREENhouse.

(B) There is a man in the greenHOUSE.

(C) The GREENhouse is in a city.

(D) There are a lot of flowers around the greenHOUSE.

乙回答：(A) The plants are all in the GREENhouse.

這是情態題，該注意的情態為：greenhouse, plants 等。

播音內容

3. Which of the following answers best describe the picture?

(A) The passage is written in French.

(B) The passage is written in bold FACE.

(C) "Like this, and this" are written in BOLDface.

(D) The passage is written by a man with bold FACE.

3. 下述那個是描述這圖片最好的答案？

(A) 這篇文章是用法語寫的。

(B) 這篇文章是寫在醒目的臉上。

(C) 「喜歡這個，還有這個」都用黑體字。

(D) 這篇文章是一名男子用粗體寫的。

4. Which of the following answers best describe the picture?

　(A) It's a bold FACE of woman.

　(B) It's a bold FACE of man.

　(C) The bold FACE has long hair.

　(D) The bold FACE wears long beard.

4. 下述那個是描述這圖片最好的答案？

　(A) 它是一張女人醒目的臉。

　(B) 它是一張男人醒目的臉。

　(C) 醒目的臉上有長長的頭髮。

　(D) 醒目的臉上戴著長長的鬍鬚。

5. Which of the following answers best describe the picture?

　(A) The plants are all in the GREENhouse.

　(B) There is no one in the GREENhouse.

　(C) The GREENhouse is full of plants.

　(D) There are a lot of flowers in the greenHOUSE.

5. 下述那個是描述這圖片最好的答案？

　(A) 所有的植物在溫室裡。

　(B) 沒有人在溫室裡。

　(C) 溫室裡放滿了植物。

　(D) 綠色的屋子裡有大量的花朵。

6. Which of the following answers best describe the picture?

(A) The plants are all in the GREENhouse.

(B) There is a man in the greenHOUSE.

(C) The GREENhouse is in a city.

(D) There are a lot of flowers around the greenHOUSE.

6. 下述那個是描述這圖片最好的答案？

(A) 所有植物在溫室裡。

(B) 有一個人在綠色的屋子裡。

(C) 溫室在一個城市裡。

(D) 有很多的花朵在綠色的屋子的周圍。

甲個別播放每題 ABCD 四選項，每播完一項暫停，再複誦：

7. Which of the following answers best describe the picture?

(A) The cowboys are chasing sheep and cattle.

(B) The cowboys are herding Cattle and sheep on the GREENbelt.

(C) It's raining on the GREENbelt.

(D) There is nothing on the green BELT.

乙回答：(B) The cowboys are herding Cattle and sheep on the GREENbelt.

> 這是動作題，該注意的動作為：herd，其他該注意的是情態：greenbelt, cowboys, cattle, sheep 等。

8. Which of the following answers best describe the picture?

(A) The karate fighter is in a suit.

(B) The fighter has a karate green BELT.

(C) The karate fighter wears a glove.

(D) The karate fighter is on a GREENbelt.

乙回答：(B) The fighter has a karate green BELT.

> 這是情態題，該注意的情態為：greenbelt, karate fighter 等。

9. Which of the following answers best describe the picture?

(A) The basketball player is in swimsuit.

(B) The basketball player is in boots.

(C) There are a pair of HIGHtop sneakers by the player.

(D) The basketball player is on the high TOP.

乙回答：(C) There are a pair of HIGHtop sneakers by the player.

> 這是情態題，該注意的情態為：basketball player, hightop, sneakers 等。

10. Which of the following answers best describe the picture?

(A) The woman is cheering on the high TOP.

(B) The woman is flying in the sky.

(C) There is nothing on the high TOP.

(D) The woman is in HIGHtop.

> 這是情態題，該注意的情態為：woman, high top, 也有動作如：cheering 等。

乙回答：(A) The woman is cheering on the high TOP.

播音內容

7. Which of the following answers best describe the picture?

(A) The cowboys are chasing sheep and cattle.

(B) <u>The cowboys are herding cattle and sheep on the GREENbelt.</u>

(C) It's raining on the GREENbelt.

(D) There is nothing on the green BELT.

7. 下述那個是描述這圖片最好的答案？

(A) 牛仔們正在追逐牛和羊。

(B) 牛仔在綠地上放牧牛羊。

(C) 綠地上在下雨。

(D) 綠地上什麼也沒有。

8. Which of the following answers best describe the picture?

(A) The karate fighter is in a suit.

(B) <u>The fighter has a karate green BELT.</u>

(C) The karate fighter wears a glove.

(D) The karate fighter is on a GREENbelt.

8. 下述那個是描述這圖片最好的答案？

(A) 空手道選手身穿西裝。

(B) 這位選手有空手道綠帶。

(C) 空手道選手戴著一副手套。

(D) 空手道選手在一片綠地上。

9. Which of the following answers best describe the picture?

  (A) The basketball player is in swimsuit.

  (B) The basketball player is in boots.

  (C) There are a pair of HIGH top sneakers by the player.

  (D) The basketball player is on the high TOP.

9. 下述那個是描述這圖片最好的答案？

  (A) 籃球運動員穿著泳裝。

  (B) 籃球運動員穿著靴子。

  (C) 球員穿著一雙高筒運動鞋。

  (D) 籃球運動員在高山的山頂上。

10. Which of the following answers best describe the picture?

  (A) The woman is cheering on the high TOP.

  (B) The woman is flying in the sky.

  (C) There is nothing on the high TOP.

  (D) The woman is in HIGH top.

10.下述那個是描述這圖片最好的答案？

  (A) 那女人在高山的山頂上歡呼。

  (B) 那女人在天空飛。

  (C) 在高山的山頂上什麼也沒有。

  (D) 那女人穿著高筒鞋。

WEEK 2

朗讀特訓篇

WEEK 2 朗讀特訓篇

DAY 1 MONDAY

朗讀短文 ❶

　　請先利用 1 分鐘的時間閱讀下面的短文，然後在 3 分鐘內以正常的速度，清楚正確的朗讀下面的短文。

Taiwan's democracy has been treading down a rocky road, but now it has finally won the chance to enter a smoother path. During that difficult time, political trust was low, political maneuvering was high, and economic security was gone. Support for Taiwan from abroad had suffered an all-time low. Fortunately, the growing pains of Taiwan's democracy did not last long compared to those of other young democracies. Through these growing pains, Taiwan's democracy matured as one can see by the clear choice the people made at this critical moment. The people have chosen clean politics, an open economy, ethnic harmony, and peaceful cross-strait relations to open their arms to the future.

　　Above all, the people have rediscovered Taiwan's traditional core values of benevolence, righteousness, diligence, honesty,

---

❶　全民英檢口說測驗中級的題型，一般是以一分鐘閱讀，兩分鐘朗讀兩段短文，也就是平均每篇短文要以一分鐘朗讀完畢。本書多加了一段短文，也就是再加半分鐘的閱讀與一分鐘的朗讀時間。

generosity and industriousness. This remarkable experience has let Taiwan become "a beacon of democracy to Asia and the world." We, the people of Taiwan, should be proud of ourselves. The Republic of China is now a democracy respected by the international community.

Yet we are still not content. We must better Taiwan's democracy, enrich its substance, and make it more perfect. To accomplish this, we can rely on the Constitution to protect human rights, uphold law and order, make justice independent and impartial, and breathe new life into civil society. Taiwan's democracy should not be marred by illegal eavesdropping, arbitrary justice, and political interference in the media or electoral institutions. All of us share this vision for the next phase of political reform.

（中譯文在本節末頁）

　　我們在第一週的看圖聽解加上複誦練習只是很簡短的單句練習，可說是為口說測驗初步的暖身了，但要發展成可以因應較長的看圖敘述或問答，則必須先多練習較長的朗讀練習。如果發音要領尚未成熟就接受看圖問答，甚至更長的敘述考驗，就必然已經輸在起跑點上了。正好英檢或多益在口說測驗的第一部分都是先要求朗讀，我們可以就練習英檢或多益朗讀測驗的題型，加強以後問答及較長敘述的能力。所以我們剛才就已模擬英檢朗讀的題型做一次練習。朗讀時最好把自己的聲音錄下來，再與母語人士所朗讀的發音比較。

　　口說能力測驗的標準在單字的發音正確以及句子的語調正確，字唸錯會使人誤解，如 snack（點心）與 snake（蛇）混淆不清時所造成的誤解就很大，重音唸錯者如 GREENhouse（溫室）與 green HOUSE（綠色的屋子）也是很大的誤解（有關單字讀音混淆還有許多解析，可以在稍後章節中進一步探討）。簡言之，字的發音、句的語調、以及斷句的語法就是口說的重點。從這三個重點，再來看語言訓練測驗中心的評分標準表，就可以更清楚掌握得分要領了。

級分	分數	說　明
5	100	發音清晰、正確，語調正確、自然；對應內容切題，表達流暢；語法、字彙使用自如，雖仍偶有錯誤，但無礙溝通。
4	80	發音大致清晰、正確，語調大致正確、自然；對應內容切題，語法、字彙之使用雖有錯誤，但無礙溝通。
3	60	發音、語調時有錯誤，因而影響聽者對其語意的瞭解。已能掌握基本句型結構，語法仍有錯誤；且因字彙、片語有限，阻礙表達。
2	40	發音、語調錯誤均多，朗讀時常因缺乏辨識能力而略過不讀；因語法、字彙常有錯誤，而無法進行有效的溝通。
1	20	發音、語調錯誤多且嚴重，又因語法錯誤甚多，認識之單字片語有限，無法清楚表達，幾乎無溝通能力。
0	0	未答／等同未答。

錄完自己的朗讀後，請開音檔，用兩部機器分別播放自己的發音與母語人士的發音來對照。然後再從頭撥一次音檔，按下文斜線 "/ " 按暫停，然後複誦。 🎧 **Mp3 012**

Taiwan's democracy / has been treading down a rocky road, / but now it has finally won the chance / to enter a smoother path. / During that difficult time, / political trust was low, / political maneuvering was high, / and economic security was gone. / Support for Taiwan from abroad / had suffered an all-time low. / Fortunately, / the growing pains of Taiwan's democracy / did not last long / compared to those of other young democracies. / Through these growing pains, / Taiwan's democracy matured as one can see / by the clear choice the people / made at this critical moment. / The people have chosen clean politics, / an open economy, / ethnic harmony, / and peaceful cross-strait relations / to open their arms to the future.

Above all, / the people have rediscovered / Taiwan's traditional core values / of benevolence, / righteousness, diligence, / honesty, generosity and industriousness. / This remarkable experience has let Taiwan / become "a beacon of democracy to Asia and the world. / "We, / the people of Taiwan, / should be proud of ourselves. / The Republic of China / is now a democracy / respected by the international community.

Yet we are still not content. / We must better Taiwan's democracy, / enrich its substance, and make it more perfect. / To accomplish this, / we can rely on the Constitution to protect human rights, / uphold law and order, / make justice independent and impartial, / and breathe new life into civil society. / Taiwan's democracy should not be marred by illegal eavesdropping, / arbitrary justice, / and political interference / in the media or electoral institutions. / All of us share this vision / for the next phase / of political reform.

分段模仿朗讀完畢之後，自己重頭再朗讀一遍，注意原來停頓的地方" / "要停 0.5 秒，一般的朗讀最少在標點符號的地方要停頓 .05 秒，聽者才知道所讀的語意告一小段落，但是若句子太長時，就須在每個介系詞片語前停頓半秒，如：

Taiwan's democracy should not be marred by illegal eavesdropping, / arbitrary justice, / and political interference / in the media or electoral institutions.

句子的構成決不是一個字一個字的唸，而是一個片語一個片語的唸，所以唸出來的音是否正確，就可以從朗讀時所停頓的位置來區別正確與否。如 I am writing to you/ to say how much/ I love your program.（" / "表示很短的停頓）若唸成 I am /writing to /you to say how /much I love your/program. 就造成了語法的錯誤了，顯

示朗讀者對英語語法的生疏，甚至不知道自己唸的是甚麼意思。從
" / "所區分出來的片語就可以看出語法是否正確了，因此朗讀時一定
要注意停頓的位置是否可區分出有意義的片語。

　　斷句錯誤只是在朗讀方面可以聽出語法的錯誤，其他問答以及敘
述的口說還要更進一步表現自己對語法、字彙、片語的基本能力，那
就涉及平常閱讀以及寫作的練習了，如果寫作的基本能力不足，說出
來的答案自然是錯得更多了。雖然本書只訓練聽力與口說能力，還是
要提醒讀者平常該多閱讀並且多練習造句，否則你的口說能力還是進
步有限的。

　　我們學習語言的過程開始於模仿，從語音、語調的模仿達到口語
的流暢 (fluency)，漸漸到用字和語法的正確 (accuracy)，而不是一
開始就學字怎麼寫，文法該怎麼用。想想我們自己的母語中文，是不
是生下來就學單字文法的呢？還是在我們開始學單字和文法句型的時
候，我們早已經會說話了？

　　甚至於，現在的溝通式教學法強調，我們入學以後，即使教室
內偏重單字文法語言知識的訊息交流 (transactional)，但對於會話
的學習就盡量延伸到教室外，與自身現實生活有關活絡的人際關係
(interpersonal) 的對話內容。只是太過於強調運用，而忽略了教室
內的單字文法學習，所說的話讓人聽不懂，甚至於因為人家聽不懂而
造成挫折感變得更不敢說話，那麼所謂的溝通目的仍然要落空的。

　　上一章 (Week 1 Day 1) 我們已經檢討過了造成聽力困難的八大因素，這一節我們也要檢討造成口語困難的八大因素 ❷，不過其因素與聽力是一致的，再從口語角度簡述：

1. 溝通互動的：

　　本書所練習的重點，都設計與真人對象的對話，沒有對象的講話，會剝奪說話技巧中最豐富的成分。而朗讀的練習雖然是不需要對象的，卻仍然要注意設想真實情境時朗讀的口氣，例如這一節所練習的範文是政府的公告文書，朗讀時就必須莊重。若是朗讀一段留言或書信，就必須像與真正對象說話一樣的口氣，若內容是私人情誼，就要用柔和、關心的語調，若是公事文書也就要莊重了。

2. 群組法的障礙：

　　我們平常說話都是一句一句說，而不是逐字唸的，所以流暢的口語也是以片語形式流露出來的，這一點我們在口說第一部分朗讀訓練時就該特別注意，錯誤的停頓也就造成了錯誤的片語，破壞了正確的語意，當然切忌逐字朗讀，也不能唸太快。

3. 贅語的障礙：

　　贅語其實是你聽懂對方的線索。說者大可以利用贅語把他們真正要說的意思說清楚。但是問答測驗時，不會聽到贅語，也不太允許你說太多贅語。

4. 簡化詞語：

　　縮寫、省略、母音減弱等簡化現象 (I will = I'll; Did you eat yet? = Dijjtyet)，都是口語中需要常練習的，不能運用這些技巧，口語就很難流暢。

---

❷　原則導向的教學法，317 頁 -321 頁，施玉惠等譯，東華，台北，2003。

5. 表達的變項：

　　口語充滿了遲疑、錯誤的開始 (false start)、停頓 (pause)、修正 (correction) 等等現象可以讓說者邊說邊想。學者有必要多熟習停頓和遲疑，如 uh, um, well, you know, I mean, like 等來填入對話中的沈默中。這是測驗以外我們用在實際環境時的差異，實際運用時，並沒有時間的限制，若你仍然死板的用測驗的經驗來與真人會話，就可能緊張而說不出話來。

6. 口語體：

　　英檢測驗中也會出現"It rains cats and dogs"（大雨滂沱）；"He has a sweet tooth"（他愛吃甜食）；"he is under weather"（他不舒服）這類的俗語，平日要多多記誦，才能講得好。

7. 說話速度：

　　若覺得外國人說話太快，想想自己說母語也是一樣的。因此多模仿人家快的地方省略了、減弱了哪些音，就可以慢慢克服障礙。所以我們要練習正確的停頓唸法，一方面練習自己適中的速度，一方面體會母語縮、弱、節音的要領，來改善自己太慢的缺點。

8. 重音、節奏、與語調：

就剛才朗讀過的短文中，請播音檔並複誦這些字（特別注意音標上重音 "ˋ" 的位置）：　🔊 **Mp3 013**

democracy	[dɪˋmkrəsi]	particular	[pɚˋtikjələ]
individual	[ˌɪndəˋvidʒuəl]	historic	[hisˋtɔrik]
milestone	[ˋmailˌston]	treading down	[ˋtrɛdiŋ ˋdaun]

　　一個字裡的各音節中有加重音節，一句中的各字中也有加高音字。音調較高的就是那一句的內容字 (content words)，也就是表達文意的字，要加高音調。其他如連接詞 or, then, and, but 或介系詞 in, on, of, to 等等，以及人稱代名詞 you, they, he 等等就要輕聲，以剛才朗讀過的句子為例：（播音檔複誦）🔊 **Mp3 012**

Taiwan's democracy has been treading down a rocky road

　　此外上一節我們已經練習過下面一些句子，同樣的 V+ing+O 的片語重音在前在後會形成完全不同的意思，現在不妨再練習一次，體會一下同樣的兩個字，除了意思不同之外，其文法的含意也不同，前一句是動名詞用法，形容後一字的功能；後一句是分詞用法，後一字是他的受詞：（播音檔複誦）🔊 **Mp3 005**

They're drying cloths. 那些是用來擦乾的布。
They're drying cloths. 他們正在把布弄乾。

They're hiking trails. 那些是步道。
They're hiking trails. 他們正在步道上散步。

They're planning meetings. 那些是為計畫而開的會議。
They're planning meetings. 他們正在計畫開會。

They're racing bikes. 那些是比賽用自行車。
They're racing bikes. 他們正在比賽自行車。

They're sailing ships. 那些是大帆船。

They're sailing ships. 他們正在揚帆行駛。

They're advertising companies. 那些是廣告公司。

They're advertising companies. 他們正在做公司的廣告。

They're mailing envelopes. 那些是郵寄用的信封。

They're mailing envelopes. 他們正在寄送信封。

They're cutting boards. 那些是砧板。

They're cutting boards. 那些機器正在切割木板。

實用單字片語

1. tread [trɛd]　*vt. & vi.*　踩，踏

   tread down 踏實，踏平，抑制（感情），壓服

   treading down a rocky road 不只是走過顛簸之路，還有踏平顛簸之路的含意。

2. 【英】maneuver [mə`nuːvə]【美】 manoeuvre [məˌnuvəˈ]　*n.*
   熟練 [謹慎] 的動作，策略，巧計，花招，軍事演習

3. critical [`kritikḷ]　*adj.*　批判的，愛挑剔別人的，危機的，危急的；決定性的

4. ethnic [`ɛθnik]　*adj.*　種族集團的成員

5. benevolence [bə`nɛvələns]　*n.*　仁慈，善心，善意

6. righteousness [`raitʃəsnis]　*n.*　正直的，正義的；正當的

7. diligence [ˈdɪlədʒəns]　*n.*　勤勉，勤奮

8. industriousness [inˈdʌstriəsnis]　*n.*　勤勉，勤奮，勤勞

   industrious [inˈdʌstriəs]　*adj.*　勤勉的，勤奮的，勤勞的

9. content [kənˈtɛnt]　*adj.*　滿足的，滿意的；甘願的

10. rely [riˈlai]　*vi.*　依靠，依賴

    rely on/upon 依靠，信賴

11. uphold [ʌpˈhold]　*vt.*　舉起，高舉

12. impartial [imˈpɑrʃəl]　*adj.*　不偏不倚的，公正的，無偏見的

13. breathe [bri ð]　*vt. & vi.*　呼吸；呼氣；吸氣

    breathe...into... 向…注入（新內容等），賦與…以（生氣等）

14. mar [mɑr]　*vt.*　毀損；損傷；玷汙（　*pt.*　&　*pp.*　marred）

    n.　汙點；缺點

15. eavesdrop [ˈivzˌdrɑp]　*vi.*　偷聽　*n.*　屋簷上流下來的水

    eavesdropping [ˈivzˌdrɑpiŋ]　*n.*　偷聽

16. arbitrary [ˈɑrbəˌtrɛri]　*adj.*　隨心所欲的，武斷的

    arbitrary justice 隨心所欲的，武斷的司法也就成了「選擇性辦案」

17. interference [ˌintəˈfirəns]　*n.*　阻礙，干涉

口說內容中文原文（馬英九總統就職演說）

我們的民主走過了一段顛簸的道路，現在終於有機會邁向成熟的坦途。在過去這一段波折的歲月裡，人民對政府的信賴跌到谷底，政治操作扭曲了社會的核心價值，人民失去了經濟安全感，台灣的國際支持也受到空前的折損。值得慶幸的是，跟很多年輕的民主國家相比，我們民主成長的陣痛期並不算長，台灣人民卻能展現日趨成熟的民主風範，在關鍵時刻，作出明確的抉擇：人民選擇政治清廉、經濟開放、族群和諧、兩岸和平與迎向未來。

尤其重要的是，台灣人民一同找回了善良、正直、勤奮、誠信、包容、進取這一些傳統的核心價值。這一段不平凡的民主成長經驗，讓我們獲得了「台灣是亞洲和世界民主的燈塔」的讚譽，值得所有台灣人引以為傲。顯然，中華民國已經成為一個受國際社會尊敬的民主國家。

不過，我們不會以此自滿。我們要進一步追求民主品質的提升與民主內涵的充實，讓台灣大步邁向「優質的民主」：在憲政主義的原則下，人權獲得保障、法治得到貫徹、司法獨立而公正、公民社會得以蓬勃發展。台灣的民主將不會再有非法監聽、選擇性辦案、以及政治干預媒體或選務機關的現象。這是我們共同的願景，也是我們下一階段民主改革的目標。

DAY 2 TUESDAY

上一節我們練習的是全民英檢口說測驗中級的題型，一般是以一分鐘閱讀，兩分鐘朗讀兩段短文，也就是平均每篇短文要以一分鐘朗讀完畢。這一節我們則介紹多益的朗讀測驗題型，多益口說測驗共 11 題，前兩題就是朗讀。一般是測兩段短文，每段短文（約 55-70 字）先閱讀準備 45 秒，然後要在 45 秒內朗讀完畢。

朗讀時最好把自己的聲音錄下來，再與母語人士所朗讀的發音比較。 Mp3 014

Directions: In this part of the test, you will read aloud the text on the screen. You will have 45 seconds to prepare. Then you will have 45 seconds to read the text aloud.

Question 1 of 11

The park is located in a quiet mountain valley where a clear stream wanders through. Stroll along the trail and you will see layers of unsophisticated paddy fields while birds sing in harmony with the flowing waters. Between late summer and early autumn, blooming wild ginger lilies turn this place into an aromatic white paradise on earth.

Directions: In this part of the test, you will read aloud the text on the screen. You will have 45 seconds to prepare. Then you will have 45 seconds to read the text aloud.

Question 2 of 11

The Teenagers' Institute at a National University in Taiwan released a survey yesterday on teenagers' favorite form of entertainment. In this survey, 2,100 teenagers in Taipei City were interviewed. 39% of the respondents say that they spend most of their free time playing computer games. 30% of the teenagers taking the survey say they like to go to movies or concerts.

【Day 2】
Tuesday

錄完自己的朗讀後，請開音檔，用兩部機器分別播放自己的發音與母語人士的發音來對照。然後再從頭撥一次音檔，按下文斜線"/"按暫停，然後複誦。

The park is located / in a quiet mountain valley / where a clear stream wanders through. / Stroll along the trail / and you will see layers / of unsophisticated paddy fields / while birds sing in harmony / with the flowing waters. / Between late summer and early autumn, / blooming wild ginger lilies / turn this place into an aromatic white paradise on earth.

＊　　　　　＊　　　　　＊

The Teenagers' Institute / at a National University in Taiwan / released a survey yesterday / on teenagers' favorite form of entertainment. / In this survey, / 2,100 teenagers in Taipei City / were interviewed. / 39% of the respondents say that / they spend most of their free time / playing computer games. / 30% of the teenagers taking the survey / say they like to go to movies or concerts.

分段模仿朗讀完畢之後，自己重頭再朗讀一遍，注意原來停頓的地方" / "要停 0.5 秒，一般的朗讀最少在標點符號的地方要停頓 0.5 秒，聽者才知道所讀的語意告一小段落，但是若句子太長時，就須在每個介系詞片語前停頓半秒，如：

The park is located / in a quiet mountain valley / where a clear stream wanders through.

這樣練習了一回英檢，一回多益的朗讀之後，我們該要問從語音、語調的模仿之後，如何達到口語的流暢 (fluency)，漸漸到用字和語法的正確 (accuracy)。我們該回顧一下第一章看圖辨義的練習成果，看看我們是如何先練習聽力，然後模仿單句的發音，進而在這一章又模仿整段的發音，大家應該很急著想如何可以不再模仿而直接可以自己表達自己想說的英語了。其實在模仿的過程中，大家已經隨著母語人士的發音，潛移默化的體會著自己表達的感覺了。但若只是模仿，就有可能發音很好，但是別人聽不懂。這就必須自己先試著說，然後聽正確的說法來比較。這過程就像我們先測驗口說，然後再聽母語來對照自己的發音一樣。不過這個口說與對照的練習我們以後的章節會做，現在不必太急，以免適應不良。現在要做的是把剛才模仿過的內容，自己不靠答案獨立的表達一下自己的答案。由於我們第一章練的是看圖辨義，下一章還會練習看圖敘述，所以現在就現學現賣把模仿過的內容自己牛刀小試一下，本書還特別把朗讀過的內容找好了對應的圖片，讓你既可以有圖像的參考，又可以為下一章的練習暖身，那還等甚麼？

　　剛才第一段朗讀的主題是一個公園，所以圖片標示 The park；第二個主題是一項調查報告，所以主題標示是 The survey。可以與同伴就這兩張圖片互相聆聽對圖片的描述，藉著剛朗讀過的記憶，再表達應該不難的。

如果實在想不起來朗讀過的內容，那就參考一下圖片下方的中文翻譯試試。

The park

The survey

這公園坐落在一個安靜的山谷中，一條清澈的小溪蜿蜒而過。在小徑上漫步，可看到原始梯田與溪谷之中，而鳥鳴與潺潺水聲諧奏著。夏末秋初時分，處處盛開的白色野薑花，把這裡妝點成芬芳繽紛的人間仙境。

台灣某大學的青少年研究所，昨天對青少年最喜歡的娛樂形式，發佈調查報告。在這個調查中，臺北市的 2,100 位青少年接受了採訪。39% 的受訪者表示，他們大部分休閒時間用來玩電腦遊戲。30% 受訪的青少年說他們喜歡去看電影或音樂會。

上一節我們列出全民音檢的口說評分標準，這一節再專就朗讀的標準也列出一表。

多益朗讀的評分要求：

Pronunciation 發音			
得分	1	評語	說話者的發音多半可理解。
	2		說話者的發音一般可理解但有一些失誤。
	3		說話者的發音都是可理解的，表達流利。
Intonation and Stress 聲調與重（ㄓㄨㄥˊ、）音			
得分	1	評語	說話者的重音和語調能準確的詮釋文本。
	2		說話者對重音、停頓和音調高低的使用大致上符合文本。
	3		說話者的重音和語調完全符合文本。

參照著這個標準，我們再練習兩段多益的口說題目。最好把自己的聲音錄下來，再與母語人士所朗讀的發音比較。 **Mp3 015**

Directions: In this part of the test, you will read aloud the text on the screen. You will have 45 seconds to prepare. Then you will have 45 seconds to read the text aloud.

Question 1 of 11

From north to south, the unique rock formations of the Northeast Coast come to an end within the waves and rock forests of Beiguan. Here, cliffs standing bravely through battering waves present a uniform and graceful cuesta landform, while tofu rocks distributed over cuestas in chessboard form glow under the sun.

Directions: In this part of the test, you will read aloud the text on the screen. You will have 45 seconds to prepare. Then you will have 45 seconds to read the text aloud.

Question 2 of 11

The size of the average Japanese family has become smaller. According to a report, there were usually four people in most families thirty years ago; that is to say, parents and two children. In 2012, however, 40% of married couples usually had one child. The other 60% of the couples said they didn't want to have children. Obviously, families in Japan nowadays have fewer children than in the past.

錄完自己的朗讀後，請開音檔，用兩部機器分別播放自己的發音與母語人士的發音來對照。然後再從頭播一次音檔，按下文斜線" / "按暫停，然後複誦。

From north to south, / the unique rock formations / of the Northeast Coast / come to an end / within the waves and rock forests of Beiguan. Here, / cliffs standing bravely through battering waves / present a uniform and graceful cuesta landform, / while tofu rocks distributed over cuestas / in chessboard form glow under the sun.

The size of the average Japanese family / has become smaller. According to a report, / there were usually four people / in most families thirty years ago; / that is to say, / parents and two children. / In 2012, / however, / 40% of married couples usually had one child. / The other 60% of the couples said / they didn't want to have children. / Obviously, / families in Japan nowadays / have fewer children than in the past.

分段模仿朗讀完畢之後，自己重頭再朗讀一遍，注意原來停頓的地方" / "要停 0.5 秒，一般的朗讀最少在標點符號的地方要停頓 0.5 秒，聽者才知道所讀的語意告一小段落，但是若句子太長時，就須在每個介系詞片語前停頓半秒，如：

From north to south, / the unique rock formations / of the Northeast Coast / come to an end / within the waves and rock forests of Beiguan.

剛才第一段朗讀的主題是一個岩石景觀，所以圖片標示 The rock formations；第二個主題是一項調查報告，所以主題標示是 The survey。可以與同伴就這兩張圖片互相聆聽對圖片的描述，藉著剛朗讀過的記憶，再表達一次。

如果實在想不起來朗讀過的內容，那就參考一下圖片下方的中文翻譯試試。

The rock formations   The family

從北到南，東北角海岸獨特的岩石景觀，延伸到北關的石林浪濤中為止，單面山在此屹立於驚濤拍浪中，展現整齊優美的單斜脊地形，豆腐岩於斜背山上被切割得像棋盤一般，在陽光下散發光采。

日本家庭平均人數已變少。根據一份報告，三十年前，大多數家庭通常有四人；也就是說，父母和兩個孩子。然而在 2012 年，40% 的已婚夫婦通常有一個孩子。其他 60% 的夫婦說他們不想要孩子。顯然，日本的家庭現在的孩子比過去少了。

我們再練習兩段多益的口說題目。最好把自己的聲音錄下來，再與母語人士所朗讀的發音比較。 🎧 **Mp3 016**

Directions: In this part of the test, you will read aloud the text on the screen. You will have 45 seconds to prepare. Then you will have 45 seconds to read the text aloud.

Question 1 of 11

Be careful. We have a cold front coming. Tomorrow is a day to stay home if you can. There will be snow falling all day, heavy at times, and strong winds. The roads will be in a bad condition, so don't drive if you don't have to. Since it will be very cold all day and through the night, if you must go outside, don't forget the hats, scarves, and gloves. The high temperature tomorrow will be only minus one degree Celsius and the low will be minus three.

Directions: In this part of the test, you will read aloud the text on the screen. You will have 45 seconds to prepare. Then you will have 45 seconds to read the text aloud.

Question 2 of 11

Thank you for calling Bank of Taiwan. All of our representatives are busy at the moment. Please stay on the line and your call will be answered shortly. For reporting a lost credit (debit) card please press 1. For information on credit cards, please press 2. For loan application, please press 3. For personal investment plans, please press 4. To hear these selections again, please press 5.

錄完自己的朗讀後，請開音檔，用兩部機器分別播放自己的發音與母語人士的發音來對照。然後再從頭播一次音檔，按下文斜線 "/" 按暫停，然後複誦。

Be careful. / We have a cold front coming. / Tomorrow is a day to stay home if you can. / There will be snow falling all day, / heavy at times, / and strong winds. / The roads will be in a bad condition, / so don't drive if you don't have to. / Since it will be very cold all day and through the night, / if you must go outside, / don't forget the hats, / scarves, / and gloves. / The high temperature tomorrow / will be only minus one degree Celsius / and the low will be minus three.

Thank you for calling Bank of Taiwan. / All of our representatives are busy at the moment. / Please stay on the line / and your call will be answered shortly. / For reporting a lost credit (debit) card, / please press 1. / For information on credit cards, / please press 2. / For loan applications, / please press 3. / For personal investment plans, / please press 4. / To hear these selections again, / please press 5.

分段模仿朗讀完畢之後，自己從頭再朗讀一遍，注意原來停頓的地方"/ "要停 0.5 秒，一般的朗讀最少在標點符號的地方要停頓 0.5 秒，聽者才知道所讀的語意告一小段落，但是若句子太長時，就須在每個介系詞片語前停頓半秒，如：

Since it will be very cold all day and through the night, / if you must go outside, / don't forget the hats, / scarves, / and gloves.

剛才第一段朗讀的主題是一個冷鋒預報，所以圖片標示 The cold front；第二個主題是一則總機電話語音，所以主題標示是 The switch board。可以與同伴就這兩張圖片互相聆聽對圖片的描述，藉著剛朗讀過的記憶，再表達一次。

　　如果實在想不起來朗讀過的內容，那就參考一下圖片下方的中文翻譯試試。

The cold front

The switch board

| 　　小心。一股冷鋒要來了。如果可以的話，明天應該待在家裡。明天整日有雪，時有大雪與強風。道路情況將會很糟，所以沒必要不要開車。因為一天從早到晚都會很冷，如果你必須外出，別忘了帽子、圍巾和手套。明天高溫將會只有攝氏零下一度，低溫將到零下三度。 | 　　感謝您致電臺灣銀行。我們的客服代表都在忙線中。請不要掛斷，我們將盡快接聽您的電話。報失的信用卡（轉帳卡）請按 1。查詢信用卡資訊，請按 2。貸款申請，請按 3。個人投資計畫，請按 4。重聽以上選項，請按 5。 |

DAY 3 WEDNESDAY

　　我們隨著英檢與多益的「看圖辨義」與「圖片描述」聽力測驗，延伸了許多模仿和不斷的逐句覆誦。此種教學法類似**聽說教學法 (Audio-Lingual Method)**，強調語言的學習是一種習慣的養成，利用模仿。記憶和不斷的句型重覆練習，務必讓學者從中形成一種語言習慣，順利與他人溝通，達到學習的目的。但是這種方法受到質疑的正是它缺乏達成溝通目的的效果。因此目前最盛行的溝通式教學法 (Communicative Language Teaching) 著重於幫助學者如何在不同情境下使用英語並了解使用英語的功能用處。與**聽說教學法**不同的是，要幫助學者創造有意義的語言，而非習得完美的文法結構或母語人士的口音，也就是說，學習的成功與否決定在於學習者**溝通能力** (communicative competence) 的程度。其特色如下：

1. 注重經由互動而達到學習如何以英語溝通。
2. 在學習情境中使用真實生活中的語料。
3. 提供讓學者專注在英語及學習過程的機會。
4. 學者的自我經驗成為課本學習中相當重要的一環。
5. 試著讓課本學習和課本外的語言使用情境結合。

　　這些特色在以後的章節中我們都會一一體現。此外，我們也注重書本中教導的語言和書本外的語言的相互關係。在這樣的概略定義下，只要是任何能幫助學者發展在真實情境中使用的**溝通能力**的練習活動，都可設計為合理且有助益的教學活動，例如：讓學者合作並溝通的同伴活動、培養學者信心的語言流暢度活動、讓學者練習和發展語言功能的角色扮演活動，以及明智地使用文法和發音為基礎的活動。所謂的「明智地使用文法和發音為基礎的活動」，其實還是要有一定程度模仿和不斷的逐句覆誦的機械式訓練，否則發音或文法的錯誤讓人根本聽不懂，那又如何溝通？只是不能一成不變的練習而已。所以下面的練習我們利用英檢與多益的看圖測驗，進行言談的展延 (Extension of Discourse)。單獨的一個句子，除非置於一個豐富的語境之下，否則其意義是很有限的。但是幾個句子放在一起，呈現一個主題，就構成了一則言談 (discourse)，其意義得以延伸。譬如，四張圖片各造一個句子：

【Day 3】
Wednesday

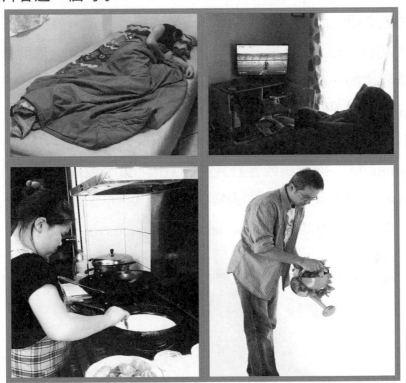

"A girl is sleeping in the bedroom." "Three boys are watching TV in the living room." "A woman is cooking in the kitchen." "A man is watering his flowers in the garden." 只是

四個獨立的句子。若將這四張圖片內容融合在一張圖片上並給予一個主題：The Johnsons' Weekend。這些句子將可連結起來，四個人物也有了關係，四個場景串聯起來，並賦予其中一個角色名字 Ann，使其有所指涉，敘述也有觀點。此時造出來的句子如下："This is weekend. Ann is sleeping in her room. Her brothers are watching TV in the living room. Her mother is cooking in the kitchen. Her father is watering his flowers in the yard." 雖然還是語言形式的練習，然而學者透過主題圖片將這四個句子作了有意義的連結，構成一項言談，不再是零碎句子的練習。言談還可以再延伸，加入邏輯的思考，呈現時間、因果或對比關係。譬如上述例子若改為 "What are there in family A and family B?" 出示兩張圖片，一張為四人的一個家庭，一張是單人的家庭。可能的句子為 "There are four members in family A **but** there's only one member in family B." "There is only one member in family B **because** she is single." 連接詞或言談連接詞 (discourse connectors)**but** 或 **because** 的出現使得造句的過程需思考，因而造出來的句子更有意義。學者要更深層的處理 (deeper-level processing) 文字。

Family A   Family B

　　這個延伸的圖片敘述活動我們也會在後面的章節練習，而這一步延伸也正是英檢與多益口說測驗要做的。

　　圖畫、地圖和圖表是一種非語言的輸入（習得）與輸出（運用）(Nonlinguistic Input and Output)，溝通式教學活動一個特質是使用「真實的」、「生活化」的「實物」作教材或教具來增進活動的真實性 (authenticity)。這些實物若與語言一同呈現時，帶給學者多種感官輸入 (multi-sensory input)。訊息透過文字圖畫或海報，甚至聲音實物，相互增強意義，增進理解。同時對文字的理解若有不足之處，非語言的圖像或聲音可予以補足。圖片或海報，亦是增進表達意義的方法。這些實物亦可作為輸出活動的提示 (cue)，例如，以看圖說故事，或討論及排列圖畫順序等。

　　下面我們就以圖示加上提示的四句主題，先朗讀句子，在試著把句子連貫成完整的敘述。

　　這樣的四句主題，是否使我們聯想起前一章所練習的圖片描述聽力測驗四個選項呢？接下來就回顧一下先前做過的看圖聽力測驗，然後利用四個選項轉為四個主題，延伸為對每張圖的完整敘述，甚至延伸為兩張圖的對比敘述。做法仍是先聽母語人士的聲音，再一一複誦，然後針對這四個主題延伸連貫成對圖片完整的敘述，自覺不足之處，再參考右頁的敘述。

Picture Description

Repeat the statements that describe the picture. 🔊 Mp3 017

1. 聽完音檔按暫停，由甲複誦下列句子，然後由乙把四句主題彙成
完整敘述。

(A) There are two signs behind the tree.

(B) The sign is behind the tree.

(C) This tree has a lamp on it.

(D) Parasols can be seen in the court.

2. 聽完音檔按暫停，由甲複誦下列句子，然後由乙把四句主題彙成
完整敘述。

(A) The man is walking far behind the car.

(B) There are hundreds of motorcycles on the street.

(C) The man is shirtless/ bare-chested.

(D) Some tattoos can be seen on the man's back.

3. 聽完音檔按暫停，由甲複誦下列句子，然後由乙把四句主題彙成
   完整敘述。

(A) The roof is planted with flowers.

(B) Three poles are on top of the roof.

(C) The crowds are near under the eaves.

(D) The day is cloudy.

4. 聽完音檔按暫停，由甲複誦下列句子，然後由乙把四句主題彙成
   完整敘述。

(A) There are four dancers on the stage.

(B) The dancers are holding red flags.

(C) The audience is paying attention to the show.

(D) One performer is playing a ring in front of the audience.

完整敘述（請播音檔） 🔊 Mp3 018

1.

There is a court in front of a restaurant. Two signs can be seen behind the tree which has a lamp on it. Tables with parasols are empty now.	一家餐館門前有一個庭院。掛著一盞燈的樹後面可以看到兩個招牌。配著陽傘的桌子現在空著。

2.

A man is shirtless/ bare-chested. Some tattoos can be seen on the man's back when walking far behind the car on the street where there are hundreds of motorcycles.	一個男人上身赤裸。可以在男人的背上見到一些紋身。他在街上的那輛車後面遠遠的走著，沿街有數百輛的摩托車。

3.

There is a wide garden planted on the whole roof. Three poles can be seen on top of the roof in the cloudy sky. The crowds are near under the eaves.	一個寬廣的花園種植在整個屋頂上。多雲的天空中可見屋頂上有三根旗杆。人群在屋簷下的附近。

4.

The audience is paying attention to the show. There are four dancers holding red flags on the stage. One performer is playing a circus ring in front of the audience.	觀眾專注看著表演。有四個舞者在舞臺上拿著紅色的旗幟。一個表演者正在觀眾面前耍弄馬戲輪圈。

5. 聽完音檔按暫停，由甲複誦下列句子，然後由乙把四句主題彙成完整敘述。

(A) The woods are far behind the river bank.

(B) The bridge is in the middle of water.

(C) There are three passengers in the center of the bridge.

(D) There is a weeping willow at the end of the bridge.

6. 聽完音檔按暫停，由甲複誦下列句子，然後由乙把四句主題彙成
   完整敘述。

(A) The cranes are behind the
   fence.
(B) There are a flock of cranes.
(C) The yard is swampy.
(D) A crane stands still.

7. 聽完音檔按暫停，由甲複誦下列句子，然後由乙把四句主題彙成
   完整敘述。

(A) Three rhinos are under the
   shade.
(B) The trees are around the
   rhinos.
(C) They are resting in the yard.
(D) Two of the rhinos are
   sleeping.

8. 聽完音檔按暫停，由甲複誦下列句子，然後由乙把四句主題彙成
完整敘述。

(A) The bridge connects mountains.

(B) The bridge stretches across the stream.

(C) The stream is far below the bridge.

(D) The bridge is in the middle of the valley.

完整敘述（請播音檔） 🔊 **Mp3 018**

5.

There is a bridge with three passengers in the middle of water. A weeping willow is at the end of the bridge. The woods are far behind the river bank.	在水中間的橋樑有三名乘客。垂柳在這座橋的盡頭。河岸遠後方是樹林。

6.

There are a flock of cranes behind the fence around the swampy yard. A crane stands still in the front.	有一群鶴在籬笆圍著的沼澤院子裡。一隻鶴靜立在前面。

7.

Three rhinos are under the shade of trees around them. They are resting in the yard and two of the rhinos are sleeping.	三隻犀牛在圍繞著他們的樹蔭下。他們在院子裡休息，其中兩隻在睡覺。

8.

The bridge connecting mountains stretches across the stream. The stream is far below the bridge in the middle of the valley.	那橋樑連接山際並橫跨溪流。那溪流在這山谷間的橋樑下方深處。

9. 聽完音檔按暫停，由甲複誦下列句子，然後由乙把四句主題彙成完整敘述。

(A) Some passengers are passing the bridge.

(B) The suspension bridge has a red tower.

(C) The bridge is hung by two cables.

(D) There are rails by the sides of the cable-stayed bridge.

10. 聽完音檔按暫停，由甲複誦下列句子，然後由乙把四句主題彙成完整敘述。

(A) The swans are swimming.

(B) The swans are following the ducks.

(C) They are crossing the river.

(D) There is an arch bridge across the river.

11-12 聽完音檔按**暫停**，由甲複誦下列句子，然後由乙把四句主題彙
成完整敘述。

What are there in beach A and beach B? Try to compare them.

A   B

A	B
1. Hot, beautiful, refreshing air.	1. The warm, golden sands, your toes.
2. Heavenly sandy beach.	2. The gentle breeze.
3. The breeze is touching every grain of sand.	3. You sit alone.
4. The sky is idyllic, blue and clear.	4. You find gorgeous, shiny shells.
5. The beautiful, big blue ocean's waves are crashing to the cliffs.	5. The shells have been washed into the shore by the rippling of the water.

完整敘述（請播音檔） 🎧 **Mp3 018**

9.

| Some passengers are passing the suspension bridge with a red tower. There are rails by the sides of the cable-stayed bridge hung by two cables. | 一些乘客路過紅塔吊橋。橋的兩側由兩條鋼索懸吊著並搭著圍欄。 |

10.

| Three swans are swimming and following four ducks. They are crossing the river under an arch bridge. | 三隻天鵝隨著四隻鴨子游過。他們正從一座拱橋下穿過。 |

11.

| Hot, beautiful, refreshing air drenches heavenly sandy beach. The breeze is touching every grain of sand. The sky is idyllic, blue and clear. The beautiful, big blue ocean's waves are crashing to the cliffs. | 炎熱、美麗、清新的空氣籠罩著天堂般的沙灘。微風撫摸著每一粒沙子。天空是那麼質樸、蔚藍、明亮。藍色大海洋美麗的海浪沖向峭壁。 |

12.

The warm, golden sand runs between your toes with the gentle breeze. As you sit alone, you find gorgeous, shiny shells that have been washed into the shore by the rippling of the water.	溫暖的、金色的沙子在柔和的微風中跑在你的腳趾之間。當你一人獨坐時，你會發現華麗、閃亮的貝殼隨著水的漣漪沖到岸邊。

Beach A has hot, beautiful, refreshing air drenching heavenly sands, while beach B carries warm, golden sand running between your toes with the gentle breeze. The breeze in beach A is touching every grain of sand because the sky is idyllic, blue and clear. In beach A, the beautiful, big blue ocean's waves are crashing to the cliffs; in beach B, as you sit alone, you find gorgeous, shiny shells that have been washed into the shore by the rippling of the water.	A 海灘炎熱、美麗、清新的空氣籠罩著天堂般的沙灘，而 B 沙灘溫暖的、金色的沙子在柔和的微風中跑在你的腳趾之間。A 海灘的微風撫摸著每一粒沙子，因為天空是那麼質樸、蔚藍、明亮。在 A 海灘，藍色大海洋美麗的海浪衝向峭壁；在 B 海灘，當你一人獨坐時，你會發現華麗、閃亮的貝殼隨著水的漣漪沖到岸邊。

做完多益圖片的敘述，我們也該試試英檢圖片的敘述，從回顧中進行新的進度，也有溫故知新的效果。

複誦每一圖畫 1 ～ 3 個該圖之描述，每題請聽錄音機播出 A、B、C、D 四個英語敘述之後，按暫停，由甲複誦四個句子，然後由乙把四句主題彙成完整敘述。自覺不足之處，再參考右頁的敘述。

Mp3 019

Descriptions 1-2

1.

A. It's cold and sunny today.

B. They're looking at a view.

C. They're wearing coats.

D. There is a beautiful reflection in the water.

2.

A. The boy has short hair.

B. The man wears a hat.

C. The girl has long hair.

D. The boy wears sport coat.

Descriptions 3

3.

A. The cup is in front of the box.

B. The red beans are filled inside the Dorayaki.

C. A wallet is behind the box.

D. There are flowers on the cup.

完整敘述（請播音檔） **Mp3 020**

1.

It's cold and sunny today and they're in coats watching a view. There is a beautiful reflection in the water.	今天寒冷而晴朗，他們穿著外套看著風景。還有美麗的倒影在水中。

2.

The boy has short hair and wears a sport coat. The man wears a hat and the girl next to him has long hair.	這個男孩是短頭髮，穿著運動外套。那人戴著一頂帽子，他身邊的女孩有一頭長髮。

3.

There is a box of Dorayaki filled with red beans. A cup with flowers is in front of the box. A wallet is behind the box.	有一整盒填滿紅豆的銅鑼燒。盒子前面有一個綴著鮮花的杯子。用鮮花的錢包是在盒子的後邊。

Descriptions 4

4.

A. The statue is facing the girl.

B. The girl is in front of the statue.

C. The TV is far next to the statue.

D. The TV is beyond the girl.

Descriptions 5-7

5.

A. She's holding a scoop.

B. She's wearing a hood.

C. She's holding a plant.

D. She's planting a tree.

6.

A. She's managing the plant.

B. She's digging the ground.

C. She's covering the dirt.

D. She's spreading the soil.

7.

A. They wear pants.

B. They are watching behind.

C. They wear sneakers.

D. They wear raincoats.

【Day 4】
Thursday

完整敘述（請播音檔） Mp3 020

4.

The girl is worshiping the statue facing her. The TV is far next to the statue beyond the girl.	這個女孩正崇拜著面對著她的雕像。電視在女孩高處遠鄰著雕像。

5.

The girl in a hood is holding a scoop in her right hand, and planting a small tree with her left hand.	戴頭套的女孩右手拿著一把鐵鍬，左手種植一棵小樹，。

6.

The girl managing the plant is digging the ground, covering the dirt by spreading the soil.	處理那棵植物的女孩正在挖地面，覆蓋泥土，鋪開土壤。

7.

The people behind the girl wearing pants and sneakers and raincoats are watching.	女孩後面穿著褲子、運動鞋和雨衣的人正在觀看。

Descriptions 8-9

8.
A. Two buckets of water.
B. They are all in T-shirts.
C. Tools on the frames.
D. Seven people.

9.
A. There're signs in the front of the classroom.
B. There's no teacher in the front of classroom.
C. On the front, you can see a black poster with signs.
D. There're posters on the wall.

Descriptions 10

10.

A. They're two beverage vending machines.

B. There are two wooden zebras in back of the scooters.

C. One of them is in front of the billboard.

D. One of them is next to the trail.

完整敘述（請播音檔） Mp3 020

8.

There are seven people in T-shirts in the room. Tools are on the frames on top of two buckets of water.	在房間有七人裡穿著 T 恤。工具架下面有兩桶水。

9.

There're signs with black poster in the front of the classroom with posters on the wall. There's no teacher in the classroom.	在教室的前面牆上的黑色海報上有標語。教室裡沒有老師。

10.

Before two beverage vending machines, there are two wooden zebras in back of the scooters. One of them is in front of the billboard and the other is next to the trail.	在兩個飲料自動販賣機前，有兩個木斑馬在摩托車後面。其中之一是在看板前和另一個在小徑旁。

Descriptions 11-12

11.

A. There is a dog in the cages.

B. The dog is in a vest.

C. Part of the cages is made of wood.

D. Part of the cages is made of steel.

12.

A. He is looking at his left.

B. He is looking at us.

C. He is looking out.

D. He is looking for company.

Descriptions 13

13.

A. They are talking to each other.

B. They are waiting to check in far from the counter.

C. They are waiting to check in an airport.

D. They are waiting behind the barricade tape.

Descriptions 14

14.

A. The car gets stuck by the side, so traffic is moving very slowly.

B. The opposite side of the highway is cleared for the traffic accident.

C. The traffic is jammed at this time of the day.

D. There's been an accident. A car has just hit the rail.

完整敘述（請播音檔） 🎧 Mp3 020

11.

There is a dog in a vest in the cages. The cages are made of wood and steel.	有一隻穿背心的狗在籠子裡。籠子是由木材和鋼做成的。

12.

The dog is looking to his left at us, and he is looking out for company.	這隻狗朝他的左邊看著我們，和他正在尋找同伴。

13.

The two men talking to each other are waiting to check in far from the counter. They are waiting to check in an airport behind the barricade tape.	互相交談的兩個男人正在櫃檯遠方等待辦理登機手續。他們在機場隔離帶後方等待報到手續。

14.

There's been an accident. The car has just hit the rail and got stuck by the side, so the traffic is moving very slowly. The opposite side of the highway is cleared for the traffic accident. The traffic is jammed at this time of the day.	出事了。這輛車剛撞上護欄，被困在路邊，所以交通非常緩慢。另一側的公路為這起交通事故淨空。這個時候，交通十分擁擠。

Descriptions 15

15.

A. We are approaching the station. Please get ready to alight.

B. When the doors are opened, please keep clear of the doors.

C. The train is arriving. Please get ready to board.

D. We are approaching the terminal station. Thank you for your patronage.

Descriptions 16

16.

A. Our school basketball team won again.

B. It was a tough game last night.

C. Their players on the other team were much taller than ours,

D. but our offense and defense were much better.

Descriptions 17

17.
A. A winter vacation is in Bali Island.
B. The weather is nice throughout the year.
C. You can get a nice tan.
D. Pack your swimsuit and sunglasses now.

完整敘述（請播音檔）　Mp3 020

15.

We are approaching the station. Please get ready to alight. When the doors open, please keep clear of the doors. This is the terminal station. Thank you for your patronage. As for the departing passengers, when the train arrives, please get ready to board after all the arriving passengers alight.

我們正在靠近車站。請準備下車。當門打開時，請保持大門的暢通。這是終點站。謝謝您的惠顧。要搭車的旅客，當火車到達，所有乘客下車後，請準備好上車。

16.

Our school basketball team won the national title the fourth year in a row. The championship game was held last night. It was a tough game. The players on the other team were much taller than ours, but our offense and defense were much better and stronger. At the bottom of the last period, the score was tied. We felt very nervous as we watched the game. Then, our player Jeremy made a Three-point shot. The crowd cheered. We had won the game!

我們學校的籃球隊連續第四年贏得了全國冠軍。昨晚舉行了決賽。這是一場硬仗。另一支球隊的球員都比我們高得多，但我們的進攻和防守都更好、更強。最後一節結束前，比數膠著。看比賽時我們感到非常緊張。接著，我們的球員傑瑞米投了一個三分球。觀眾歡呼。我們贏得了比賽！

17.

If you plan to take a vacation in winter, Bali Island in Indonesia is a great place to go. The weather is nice throughout the year, but the best time of the year is from December to April. It rains sometimes, but the rain can cool you off. You can get a nice tan. Imagine that you are enjoying the sunshine at the beach on the island while your friends are shivering in the cold at home. So, what are you waiting for? Pack your swimsuit and sunglasses for a wonderful vacation in the sun — here in Bali Island.

如果您計畫在冬天去度假，在印尼的峇厘島是一個很棒的地方。天氣很好，在全年中，但一年的最佳時間是 12 月至次年 4 月。有時會下雨，但雨可以帶來清涼。你可以曬到漂亮的褐色。想像一下你在享受著島上海灘上的陽光，而你的朋友在家裡的寒冷中顫抖著。所以，你還在等什麼呢？收拾起你的游泳衣和太陽鏡，準備享受在峇厘島太陽下的一個精彩假期。

前兩節我們以聽力測驗的圖片練習敘述的口說能力，都是直接對圖片做簡單或延伸的敘述，雖然針對英檢的看圖敘述以及多益的圖片描述是很直接實用的暖身活動，但是英檢口說還有回答問題的測驗，而多益也還有問答與申論的測驗，我們不妨利用前一章最後一節的聽力題目，來練習看圖問答，甚至看圖申論，已彌補這方面的活動。在這裡我們還是以朗讀練習為主，以簡單的問答複誦母語人士的發音，進一步的延伸活動我們留待下一章「看圖敘述」再練習。

Picture Description
with Questions and Responses

（打開音檔，甲複誦每一問題後按暫停，待乙回答後再聽下一問題答問，若乙自覺不足，再參考右頁母語音檔朗讀一次） 🎧 **Mp3 021**

1.

1. 甲一問乙一答：

(A) What is the boy doing?

(B) What is the boy wearing?

(C) What is the girl doing?

(D) What is the girl wearing?

乙回答：＿＿＿＿＿＿＿＿＿

＿＿＿＿＿＿＿＿＿＿＿＿＿

2.

2. 甲一問乙一答：

(A) Where are the people?

(B) What are the people doing?

(C) What are the people wearing?

(D) What are they waiting for?

乙回答：＿＿＿＿＿＿＿＿

＿＿＿＿＿＿＿＿＿＿＿

3.

3. 甲一問乙一答：

(A) What does the girl wear?

(B) What is the girl cooking with?

(C) What is the girl stirring?

(D) What do you think she is cooking?

乙回答：＿＿＿＿＿＿＿＿

＿＿＿＿＿＿＿＿＿＿＿

【Day 5】 Friday

（請播音檔） Mp3 022

1. 乙回答：

(A) The boy is crying.
(B) The boy is wearing a cowboy hat.
(C) The girl is smiling.
(D) The girl is wearing a hat.
(A) 男孩在哭。
(B) 男孩戴著一頂牛仔帽子。
(C) 女孩微笑。
(D) 女孩戴著一頂帽子。

2. 乙回答：

(A) The people are in an arcade by the classroom.
(B) They are waiting for something.
(C) They wear T-shirts.
(D) They are waiting for the class.
(A) 人們在教室的騎樓裡。
(B) 他們正在等待著某事。
(C) 他們穿著 T 恤。
(D) 他們等待上課。

3. 乙回答：

(A) The girl wears an apron.

(B) The girl is cooking with a pan.

(C) The girl is stirring soup.

(D) She is cooking vegetable soup.

(A) 那個女孩穿了一條圍裙。

(B) 這個女孩正在用一個平底鍋烹製。

(C) 女孩正在攪拌湯。

(D) 她在煮蔬菜湯。

4.

4. 甲一問乙一答：

(A) Where is the path leading to?

(B) Have you been there before?

(C) What are behind the waterfall?

(D) How does it feel like in the waterfall?

乙回答：＿＿＿＿＿＿＿＿

＿＿＿＿＿＿＿＿＿＿＿＿

5.

5. 甲一問乙一答：

(A) What are the trees made of?

(B) What are the trees bound with?

(C) What do you think the trees are for?

(D) What are behind the trees?

乙回答：＿＿＿＿＿＿＿

＿＿＿＿＿＿＿＿＿＿＿＿＿

6.

6. 甲一問乙一答：

(A) Where is the playground?

(B) Where are the ladders leading to?

(C) Have you played with the swings?

(D) Why isn't there anybody?

乙回答：＿＿＿＿＿＿＿

＿＿＿＿＿＿＿＿＿＿＿＿＿

7.

7. 甲一問乙一答：

(A) What is the stilt walker doing to the crowds?

(B) What is the stilt walker holding?

(C) What is the woman doing to him?

(D) How are the crowds reacting?

乙回答：_____

_____

4. 乙回答：

(A) The path leads to the waterfall.

(B) Yes. I have been there before.

(C) A cave is behind the waterfall.

(D) It feels like in a shower.

(A) 這條小路通向瀑布。

(B) 是。我以前去過那裡。

(C) 一個洞穴在瀑布的後面。

(D) 感覺就像在淋浴。

5. 乙回答：

(A) The trees are made of bamboo.

(B) The trees are bound with barrier tape.

(C) I think the trees are a sign for gingko trees.

(D) There are gingko trees behind the sign.

(A) 樹由竹子製成。

(B) 樹木被隔離帶綁著。

(C) 我認為那樹是銀杏樹的標誌。

(D) 標誌背後是銀杏樹。

6. 乙回答：

(A) The playground is in the woods.

(B) The ladders lead to the woods.

(C) Yes. I have played with the swings.

(D) Because it is going to rain.

(A) 遊樂場在樹林裡。

(B) 階梯進入樹林裡。

(C) 是。我玩過那些鞦韆。

(D) 因為要下雨了。

7. 乙回答：

(A) The stilt walker is performing to the crowds.

(B) The stilt walker is holding an umbrella.

(C) The woman is taking a picture of him.

(D) The crowds are paying attention on him.

(A) 高蹺人正表演給群眾看。

(B) 高蹺人撐著傘。

(C) 那女人正在拍他的照片。

(D) 群眾關注他的表演。

8.

8. 甲一問乙一答：

(A) What is the statue wearing?

(B) Is that Super Mario?

(C) Why do they hold it on the street?

(D) What are the people lifting him wearing?

　　乙回答：＿＿＿＿＿＿＿＿

　　＿＿＿＿＿＿＿＿＿＿＿＿

9.

9. 甲一問乙一答：

(A) What is the woman doing?

(B) What is the woman wearing?

(C) What is the woman riding?

(D) What is behind the woman?

　　乙回答：＿＿＿＿＿＿＿＿

　　＿＿＿＿＿＿＿＿＿＿＿＿

10.

10. 甲一問乙一答：

(A) What are people playing behind basketball stands?

(B) Are they playing basketball?

(C) What do you think the man standing by the basketball stands is doing?

(D) What are hanging above the court?

乙回答：＿＿＿＿＿＿＿＿＿

＿＿＿＿＿＿＿＿＿＿＿＿＿＿＿

8. 乙回答：

(A) The statue wears suspender trousers.

(B) Yes. It is Super Mario.

(C) They hold it on the street for a parade.

(D) The people lifting him are wearing diapers.

(A) 這座雕像穿著吊帶褲。

(B) 是，它是超級馬利歐。

(C) 他們舉著馬利歐在街上遊行。

(D) 舉著他的人都穿著尿布

9. 乙回答：

(A) The woman is on a parade.

(B) The woman is wearing a fancy hat.

(C) The woman is riding a float.

(D) A classical Chinese building is behind the woman.

(A) 那女人在一個遊行上。

(B) 那女人帶著精美的帽子。

(C) 那女人搭著一輛花車。

(D) 那女人的背後是一座古典的中國建築。

10. 乙回答：

(A) The people are gathering behind the basketball stand.

(B) No. They are not playing basketball.

(C) The man standing by the basketball stands is waiting his children.

(D) There banners hanging on the court.

(A) 他們正聚集在籃球架後面。

(B) 不，他們沒在打籃球。

(C) 站籃球架旁的人正在等他的孩子。

(D) 許多旗幟掛在球場上。

WEEK 3

看圖敘述篇

WEEK 3 看圖敘述篇

上一章我們最後以多益的看圖聽解練習朗讀，這一章我們打鐵趁熱就直接練習多益的圖片描述題型。多益圖片描述的要求是：30 秒準備時間，45 秒以內敘述完畢，盡可能的描述圖內一切細節，圖片大致屬於休閒活動、飲食、娛樂、健康、家事、採購逛街、旅遊、街景等等。我們看看多益的圖片描述評分標準：

得分			
	3	評語	描述符合圖片，包含細節。
			說話者幾乎都能流暢符合，可容易聽懂。
			說話者的詞彙準確符合圖片。
			說話者的結構連貫一致。
	2	評語	說話者描述符合圖片，但遺漏重要內容，偏重於小細節。
			說話者一般能流暢符合，但有一些不容易聽懂。
			說話者詞彙不足以符合圖片，偶爾錯誤。
			說話者的結構不連貫阻礙整體理解。
	1	評語	說話者只能描述部分圖片，難以表達概念。
			說話者停頓過久，經常遲疑，不易聽懂。
			說話者詞彙錯誤且經常重複相同字彙。
			說話者的結構嚴重阻礙整體理解。
	0		毫無發音或發音與問題無關。

根據上述標準，我們可以發現大致符合看圖聽解的預判重點，而這些重點也就是我們要敘述的重點：

1. 對圖片上的人物，要注意：

A. 他們在做甚麼（what）？在哪裡（where）？

B. 他們是誰（who）？是否穿甚麼制服或拿甚麼工具顯示他們的身份。

C. 如何區別他們（what）？注意有無特殊的服飾、髮型、眼鏡、帽子等等。

D. 表情如何（how）？喜怒哀樂等等。

2. 對圖片上的靜物，要注意：那是甚麼東西（what）？甚麼材質（what is it made of）？在做甚麼？以及在甚麼地方等等。

3. 對圖片上的場景，注意：在哪裡？前方（in front of）有甚麼？發生甚麼事了？其背景等等。

針對上述重點，我們再複習該熟習的詞彙：

1. 位置 (where)

這種題型通常針對人與物與其他人與物位置的關係，因此有關於位置的介系詞就是我們要特別注意描述的，否則就會如上述評分標準所指出的「詞彙不足以符合圖片」問題。

（請聽錄音隨聲複誦） **Mp3 023**

above 在上（高處），**against** 對著，**among** 之間，**at** 在某點，**at the back of** 在其背面，**at the end (bottom) of** 在尾（底）端，**atop** 在頂上，**before** 之前，**behind** 後面，**below** 下面，**beneath**（緊貼）下面，**between** 之間，**by** 旁邊，**close to** 靠近，**in** 裡面，**inside** 內部，**in front of** 在前面，**near** 接近，**next to** 隔

壁，**on** 在上面，**on top of** 在上面的，**over** 在上（越過），**under** 在下（直下），等等。

關於介系詞上下關係的圖解：　　　　**at, on, in** 的空間關係：

Over	above	up
on		

Beneath		
Under	below	down

at　　　　on

in

2. 動作 (what)

第一節我們在檢討中提過動作多半是現在進行式與現在式，所以要注意同樣是動詞原型 VR+ing 的形式，卻有現在分詞與動名詞的運用的不同，這裡我們要再補充除了現在分詞所表現的主動語態 (be+V-ing)，還有過去分詞所表現的被動語態 (be+V-ed)，因此要注意常見的主動語被動分詞，否則就會如上述評分標準所指出的「一般能流暢符合，但有一些不容易聽懂」的問題。

（請聽錄音隨聲複誦）　🎧 **Mp3 024**

A. 主動

cleaning 清洗，**crossing** 越過，**cutting** 切割，**drawing** 繪圖，**drinking** 喝酒，**eating** 吃，**following** 跟隨著，**holding** 握，**jogging** 慢跑，**listening** 聽，**loading** 載，**locking** 鎖，**looking** 注視著，**making** 製作，**packing** 包裝，**playing** 玩，**pouring** 澆，**pulling** 拉，**pushing** 推，**selling** 銷售，**setting** 設置，**sitting** 坐，**speaking** 說，**stretching** 拉伸，**sweeping**

掃，**talking** 談，**typing** 打 字，**walking** 行 走，**watching** 觀看，**watering** 澆水，**working** 工作，**wrapping** 包裝，**writing** 寫……

B. 被動

　　<u>**being + cleaned**</u>（ 被 ） 打 掃，**cleared** 清 除，**displayed** 顯 示，**dug up** 挖，**handed** 遞 給，**locked** 鎖 定，**painted** 畫（漆），**planted** 種植，**poled**（用棒）支撐，**pilled** 堆，**served** 送達，**set up** 設置，**towed** 拖，**walked**（使）走，**washed** 洗，**watered** 澆水，**wrapped** 包裹……

3. 情態 how、what 和 who

　　這類題目問的是圖中事物的情況或狀態，所以要注意的是圖中的焦點並想像你自己將如何描述這個情境，通常就要用到下列的形容詞與過去分詞當形容詞的字，否則就會如上述評分標準所指出的「一般能流暢符合，但有一些不容易聽懂」的問題。

A. 形容詞（請聽錄音並複誦）　🎧 Mp3 025

　　afraid 害怕的，**asleep** 睡著了，**beautiful** 美麗的，**bent** 彎曲的，**bright** 明亮的，**clean** 乾淨的，**dark** 黑暗的，**dirty** 骯髒的，**empty** 空的，**flat** 平的，**full** 充實的，**happy** 快樂的，**heavy** 重的，**high** 高的，**light** 亮的，**long** 長的，**open** 開放的，**rainy** 多雨，**round** 圓，**tall** 高，**sad** 傷心，**straight** 直的，**wet** 濕的……

B. 過去分詞當形容詞

arranged 安排好的，blocked 被阻止的，broken 破碎的，chained 被拴著的，cleared 清空的，closed 關閉的，crowded 擠的，crushed 壓碎的，deserted 空無一人，displayed 顯示著，equipped 裝備著，loaded 載著，occupied 被佔據，parked 停泊著，piled 堆著，posted 張貼著，scattered 分散著，seated 坐著，stacked 堆積著，stranded 困著，tried 試著……

4. 同音混淆

聽力測驗中常見在錯誤的選項中用同音字來混淆正確答案，轉換成口說測驗時就變成了發音要注意不可混淆的缺點，否則就會如上述評分標準所指出的「詞彙不足以符合圖片」問題。常見類同字如下：

A. 母音近似的字（請聽錄音隨聲複誦） Mp3 026

afford / offer 負擔得起 / 出價，awful / oval 可怕 / 橢圓形，ball / bawl 球 / 哭, bike / hike 自行車 / 徒步旅行，cheer / chair 歡呼 / 椅子，clean / lean 清潔 / 傾斜，coach / couch 教練 / 沙發，hitting / fitting 打 / 配件，just / adjust 只是 / 調整，lake / rake 湖 / 耙子，lamp / ramp 燈 / 坡道，law / raw 法律 / 原材料，lean / learn 傾斜 / 學習，light / right 光 / 右，lock / rock 鎖 / 岩石，low / row 低 / 行，owl / foul 貓頭鷹 / 腐爛，mail / rail 郵件 / 鐵路，meal / wheal 餐 / 條痕，on the / under 上 / 下，peach / speech 桃 / 演講，peel / pill 皮 / 丸，pine / fine 松樹 / 好的，player / prayer 球員 / 禱告，playing

/ **plane** 播放 / 平面，**pool** / **pull** 池 / 拉，**poor** / **four** 窮人 / 四個，**possible** / **impossible** 可能 / 不可能，**rag** / **bag** 破 / 袋子，**selling** / **sailing** 銷售 / 帆船，**sheer** / **share** 純粹 / 共用，**shopping** / **chopping** 購物的 / 切著的，**talk** / **take** 談話 / 帶，**there** / **they're** 那裡 / 他們，**try** / **tie** 嘗試 / 領帶，**wait** / **weigh** 等待 / 稱重，**walk** / **work** 步行 / 工作，**west** / **rest** 西 / 休息，**wheel** / **will** 輪 / 會⋯⋯

B. 相同的字根、自首、字尾

　　aboard / **abroad** / **board** 船上 / 在國外 / 木板，**inboard** / **onboard** 船內 / 船載，**agree** / **disagree** 同意 / 不同意，**appear** / **disappear** 出現 / 消失，**aware** / **unaware** 知道 / 不知道，**close** / **enclose** 關閉 / 圍繞，**extract** / **exhale** 提取 / 呼出，**just** / **adjust** 只 / 調整，**relay** / **delay** 接替 / 延誤，**reread** / **relayed** 重讀 / 接替，**rest** / **arrest** 休息 / 逮捕，**similar** / **dissimilar** 類似 / 異種，**terrible** / **terrific** 可怕 / 很棒，**tie** / **untie** 領帶 / 解開，**tire** / **rctire** 輪胎 / 退役，**type** / **retype** 類型 / 重新輸入，**underworked** / **underused** 次要工作 / 未充分利用，**undrinkable** / **unthinkable** 不能飲用 / 不可想像⋯⋯

　　上述四個重點，固然是聽力測驗的要領，卻也是看圖敘述的重點。口說描述對於圖片中位置、動作、情境的要領是一樣的。而同音混淆的問題也一樣會在口說描述中是一項考驗，如果發音不清楚，就造成評分老師們的混淆了。此外評分標準中提到的「結構」問題，就是口說者的基本文法結構能力的問題了。這一節我們先整理語料，針對描述「位置」、「動作」、「情態」所列的詞彙，配合多益題型，練習圖片描述的字彙、介系詞、形容詞的運用。以後幾節我們進一步練習描述的計畫、組織，除字彙、介系詞、形容詞之外，再整合副詞、連接詞以及文法結構上的練習。

In	At	On	副詞
(the) bed*	class*	the bed*	downstairs
the bedroom	home	the ceiling	downtown
the car	the library*	the floor	inside
(the) class*	the office	the horse	outside
the library*	school*	the plane	upstairs
school*	work	the train	uptown

* 對這些位置，你有時可以使用不同的介系詞。

1.

2.

3.

4.

一、位置：下列句子有關於這四張圖片的描述填入適當的介系詞或片語。做完後再聽錄音複誦。

1. The dining table is _____ the lamp.

2. The two chairs are _____ the table.

3. The books are _____ the shelf.

4. There is a bowl of flowers _____ the table.

5. There is a couch _____ the table.

6. The girl is standing _____ the drum.

7. The man in a red cape is _____ the float.

8. The man in a black coat is _____ the float.

9. The boy is standing _____ the drums.

10. The two women on the bench are sitting _____ the road.

請聽錄音並複誦 🎧 **Mp3 027**

一、位置：

1. The dining table is under the lamp.

   餐桌在燈下。

2. The two chairs are at the table.

   那兩把椅子在餐桌邊。

3. The books are at the bottom of the shelf.

   書在書架上的底部。

4. There is a bowl of flowers in the middle of the table.

   有一盆花在桌子中間。

5. There is a couch behind the table.

   有一張沙發在桌子後面。

6. The girl is standing at the drum.

   這個女孩站在鼓邊。

7. The man in a red cape is beneath the float.

   那個披著紅斗篷的人在花車下方。

8. The man in a black coat is in back of the float.

   穿著黑色外套的男人在花車的後面。

9. The boy is standing by the drums.

   那個男孩站在鼓邊。

10. The two women on the bench are sitting by the road.

    坐在板凳上的兩個女人正坐在路邊。

二、動作：下列句子有關於這四張圖片的描述填入適當的分詞或片語。做完後再聽錄音複誦。

1. The two women sitting on the bench are _____ the parade.

2. The girl is _____ the drum.

3. The man in a red coat is _____ by the float.

4. The man in a black coat is _____ the road.

5. The parade is _____ its length.

6. The man in a red cape is _____ up to the float.

7. The last float is _____ the other float.

8. The boy by the drum is _____ the floor with his foot.

9. The audiences of the parade are _____ along the road.

10. There are drums _____ for the tourists.

請聽錄音並複誦 🎧 **Mp3 028**

二、動作：

1. The two women sitting on the bench are watching the parade.

   坐在板凳上的兩名婦女正在觀看遊行。

2. The girl is playing the drum.

   那個女孩正在打鼓。

3. The man in a red coat is walking by the float.

   穿紅外套男人走過花車。

4. The man in a black coat is crossing the road.

   穿黑色外套男人橫過馬路。

5. The parade is stretching its length.

   遊行隊伍伸展它的長度。

6. The man in a red cape is looking up to the float.

   披著紅斗篷的男人正仰望著花車。

7. The last float is following the other float.

   最後一輛花車跟隨著其他花車。

8. The boy by the drum is sweeping the floor with his foot.

   鼓旁那男孩用腳在掃地。

9. The audiences of the parade are scattered along the road.

   遊行的觀眾沿著這條路散佈著。

10. There are drums arranged for the tourists.

    那些鼓是為遊客安排的。

三、情態：下列句子有關於這四張圖片的描述填入適當的過去分詞或
　　形容詞。

1. With light shedding from the window, the book room is
　　_____ .

2. The top of the book shelf is _____ .

3. Without any lamps, the living room will be _____ .

4. The parade is _____ with floats.

5. The road is _____ by the parade.

6. The audiences of the parade are not _____ .

7. The two women watching the parade are _____ .

8. The bottom of the book shelf is _____ .

9. The table, bench, and couch in the living room are all
　　_____ and straight.

10. The floors in both rooms are _____ .

請聽錄音並複誦 🎧 Mp3 029

三、情態：

1. With light shedding from the window, the book room is bright.

有光線從窗戶照入，房間是光明的。

2. The top of the book shelf is empty.

書架的頂層是空的。

3. Without any lamps, the living room will be dark.

沒有燈，客廳裡就很暗。

4. The parade is equipped with floats.

遊行隊伍配備了花車。

5. The road is occupied by the parade.

這條路被遊行隊伍佔領。

6. The audiences of the parade are not crowded.

遊行隊伍的觀眾並不擁擠。

7. The two women watching the parade are seated.

兩個看遊行的女人是坐著的。

8. The bottom of the book shelf is full.

那書架底部是滿的。

9. The table, bench, and couch in the living room are all long and straight. 桌子、長椅和客廳的沙發都是長而直的。

10. The floors in both rooms are clean.

兩個房間的地板是乾淨的。

DAY **2** TUESDAY

　　這一節我們先回顧這些前章圖片敘述的句子，找出它們的主詞 (subject)、動詞 (verb)、受詞 (object) 以及補語 (complement) 等等，然後再想想自己如何延伸幾句對這張圖的新敘述，我們可以先看需要用到的字彙詞類（上一節已介紹了名詞、介系詞、形容詞，這一節我們再加上動詞與副詞），然後再試著自己造句，若自覺不足再參考右頁的範例。

1.

(A) There are two signs behind the tree.
　　　S　　V　　　SC

(B) The sign is behind the tree.
　　　S　V　　　SC

(C) This tree has a lamp on it.
　　　S　　V　　　O

(D) Parasols can be seen in the court.
　　　S　　　　V SC

造句之前，先與同伴腦力激盪一下你們會用到哪些名詞、動詞、形容詞、副詞與介系詞。

延伸參考：

全民英檢的初級口說測驗就有這樣的題型。

1.

名詞	Sign, tree, lamp, parasol, court, yard, balcony, banner, rail, fan, ceiling.
動詞	are, is, has, be, sit.
形容詞或副詞	Blue, red, empty, wooden, scattered.
介系詞	Behind, on, in, by, with.

請聽錄音並複誦 Mp3 030

There is a court in front of a shop or restaurant.

有一庭院在商店或餐廳前面。

There are many tables in the yard. 在院子裡有許多桌子。

The tables are covered with blue tablecloths.

桌子蓋著藍色的桌布。

The tables are empty. 桌子是空的。

There are parasols by the tables. 桌子邊有遮陽傘。

The court is behind a tree with a lamp.

該庭院在一棵掛著一盞燈的樹背後。

There are plants scattered around the yard.

有些植物散佈在院子周圍。

There are two men sitting on the balcony behind the black banner. 有兩個男人坐在黑色橫幅招牌後的陽臺上。

There are wooden rails around the balcony.
陽臺周圍有木製的圍欄。

There are fans on the ceiling of the balcony.
陽臺天花板上有風扇。

The men sitting on the balcony is wearing white cap.
坐在陽臺上的男子戴著白色的帽子。

There are no customers in the court. 庭院裡沒有顧客。

2.

(A) The man is walking far behind the car.
　　　S　　　V

(B) There are hundreds of motorcycles on the street.
　　　S　V　　SC

(C) The man is shirtless/ bare-chested.
　　　S　V　　　　　SC

(D) Some tattoos can be seen on the man's back.
　　　　S　　　　V　SC

　　造句之前，先與同伴腦力激盪一下你們會用到哪些名詞、動詞、形容詞、副詞與介系詞。

延伸參考：

2.

名詞	Man, hundred, motorcycle, guiding tile
動詞	Is, are, be, Look, park
形容詞或副詞	Far, shirtless/ bare-chested, ahead,
介系詞	Behind, on, along

請聽錄音並複誦 Mp3 030

The shirtless/ bare-chested man is walking between the white line and guiding tile trail.
赤裸上身的男子走在白線和導盲磚步道之間。

The two women standing ahead of the man are looking outside at the side. 站在這男人前面的兩名女人正在路邊向外看著。

Far ahead of them is a blue car on the road.

在他們前方遠處道路上是一輛藍色的車。

There are hundreds of motorcycles parked along the left side of the road. 有數百輛摩托車停在路的左側。

The motorcycles are parked along the wall.

摩托車沿著牆停放。

A long row of trees are shading the sidewalk by the wall.

靠牆一長排的樹蔭蔽著人行道。

The shirtless/ bare-chested man has tattoos on his back.

赤裸上身的男人背上有紋身。

There are red parasols on the right side of the road.

在路的右邊有紅色的遮陽傘。

There is a green sign saying "Free..." next to the parasols.

陽傘的旁邊有綠色標誌寫著「自由（免費）…」。

延伸參考：

3.

(A) The <u>roof</u> is <u>planted</u> with flowers.
　　　S　V　SC

(B) Three <u>poles</u> <u>are</u> <u>on top</u> of the roof.
　　　　　S　V　SC

(C) The <u>crowds</u> <u>are</u> <u>near under the eaves.</u>
　　　　S　V　　　SC

(D) The <u>day</u> <u>is</u> <u>cloudy.</u>
　　　S　V　SC

【Day 2】
Tuesday

　　造句之前，先與同伴腦力激盪一下你們會用到哪些名詞、動詞、形容詞、副詞與介系詞。

延伸參考：

3.

名詞	Roof, flower, pole, crowd, eave, square
動詞	Plant, are, is
形容詞或副詞	Far, shirtless/ bare-chested, ahead, across
介系詞	of, on, with

請聽錄音並複誦 Mp3 030

There is a garden of roof across the square. 屋頂花園橫過廣場。

A crowd of people are gathering on the square.

一群人正聚集在廣場上。

There are three empty poles on top of the roof.

有三支空的竿子在屋頂上。

177

The garden is planted with different colors of flowers.

花園裡種植著不同顏色的鮮花。

The whole garden is designed as rainbows across the sky.

整個花園設計為劃過天空的彩虹。

The garden of rainbows is under a cloudy sky.

彩虹的花園是在多雲的天空下。

The crowds are entering the building. 人群正在進入建築物。

The crowds are approaching the building's eaves.

人群正在接近這座建築的屋簷。

4.

(A) There are four dancers on the stage.
　　 S　 V　　　 SC

(B) The dancers are holding red flags.
　　　　 S　　　 V　　　 O

(C) The audience is paying attention to the show.
　　　　 S　　　 V　　　 O

(D) One performer is playing a circus ring in front of the
　　　　 S　　　　 V　　　　 O

audience.

　　造句之前，先與同伴腦力激盪一下你們會用到哪些名詞、動詞、形容詞、副詞與介系詞。

延伸參考：

4.

名詞	Dancer, stage, audience, flag, circus ring, performers, entertainment
動詞	Hold, pay, play
形容詞或副詞	Red, in front of
介系詞	On, to, of

請聽錄音並覆誦 🎧 **Mp3 030**

There are four performers on the stage. 有四個表演者在舞臺上。

There are four dancers holding red flags on the stage.

有四個舞者在舞臺上拿著紅色的旗幟。

The stage is in front of a Chinese classical building.

舞台在中國古典建築前。

It's winter with a cloudy day. 這是冬天多雲的天氣。

There is a performer playing with circus rings in the square.

藝人在廣場上耍馬戲圈。

The audiences are paying attention to the entertainment.

觀眾關注著娛樂表演。

五種單句的基本句型：

1. S+V（主詞＋動詞）

2. S+V+SC（主詞＋動詞＋主詞補語）

3. S+V+O（主詞＋動詞＋受詞）

4. S+V+O+OC（主詞＋動詞＋受詞＋受詞補語）

5. S+V+IO+DO（主詞＋動詞＋間接受詞＋直接受詞）

＊S：主詞　V：動詞　O：受詞　C：補語

　IO：間接受詞　DO：直接受詞

5.

[Day 2]
Tuesday

5

(A) The <u>woods</u> <u>are</u> far <u>behind the river bank.</u>
      S   V   SC

(B) The <u>bridge</u> <u>is</u> <u>in the middle</u> of water.
      S   V   SC

(C) <u>There</u> <u>are</u> three <u>passers</u> in the center of the bridge.
    S   V   SC

(D) <u>There</u> <u>is</u> a weeping <u>willow</u> at the end of the bridge.
    S   V   SC

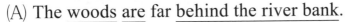

　　造句之前，先與同伴腦力激盪一下你們會用到哪些名詞、動詞、形容詞、副詞與介系詞。

延伸參考：

5.

名詞	Woods, bridge, passenger, weeping willow
動詞	Are, is
形容詞或副詞	Weeping, far, across
介系詞	Behind, in, at,

請聽錄音並覆誦 🎧 Mp3 030

The bridge is in the middle of water. 這座橋是在水中央。

There is a backpack girl by the rail in the center of the bridge.
在這座橋的中心欄杆旁有一個背背包的女孩。

There is a weeping willow at the end of the bridge.
這座橋的尾端有一棵垂柳。

A couple is facing the weeping willow. 一對情侶面向著垂柳。

The woods are far across the road by the river bank.
遠方跨過河岸邊道路是樹林。

There are venders under the woods. 樹林下有攤販。

五種單句的基本句型：

1. S+V（主詞＋動詞）
2. S+V+SC（主詞＋動詞＋主詞補語）
3. S+V+O（主詞＋動詞＋受詞）
4. S+V+O+OC（主詞＋動詞＋受詞＋受詞補語）
5. S+V+IO+DO（主詞＋動詞＋間接受詞＋直接受詞）
＊S：主詞 V：動詞 O：受詞 C：補語
IO：間接受詞 DO：直接受詞

DAY 3 WEDNESDAY

這一節我們仍如上一節回顧前章圖片敘述的句子，找出它們的主詞 (subject)、動詞 (verb)、受詞 (object) 以及補語 (complement) 等等，然後再想想自己如何延伸幾句對這張圖的新敘述，我們可以先看到需要用到的字彙詞類（名詞、介系詞、形容詞，這一節我們再加上動詞與副詞），然後再試著自己造句，若自覺不足再參考右頁的範例。

1.

(A) Some <u>passengers</u> are <u>passing</u> the <u>bridge</u>.
　　　　　　S　　　　　　V　　　　　O

(B) The <u>suspension bridge</u> <u>has</u> a red <u>tower</u>.
　　　　　　　S　　　　　　　V　　　　　O

(C) The <u>bridge</u> <u>is</u> <u>hung</u> by two cables.
　　　　　S　　V　SC

(D) <u>There</u> <u>are</u> <u>rails</u> by the sides of the cable-stayed bridge.
　　　S　　V　　SC

延伸參考：

1.

名詞	Passer, bridge, bottom, tower, cable, mesh
動詞	Are, has, link
形容詞或副詞	Suspension, red, stayed
介系詞	On, to, by, of, with

請聽錄音並覆誦 🎧 Mp3 031

There are three passers on the bridge. 橋上有三個路人。

The suspension bridge has a red tower. 懸索橋有一個紅色的塔。

The bridge is leading to a foothill / bottom of a mountain.

這座橋通往一座山腳。

The bridge is hung by two cables. 這座橋是由兩條鋼纜懸吊的。

There are rails by the sides of the cable-stayed bridge.

吊橋兩側有欄索。

The rails are linked with wires / wire mesh.

欄索上結著鐵絲網 / 孔網。

五種單句的基本句型：

1. S+V（主詞 + 動詞）

2. S+V+SC（主詞 + 動詞 + 主詞補語）

3. S+V+O（主詞 + 動詞 + 受詞）

4. S+V+O+OC（主詞 + 動詞 + 受詞 + 受詞補語）

5. S+V+IO+DO（主詞 + 動詞 + 間接受詞 + 直接受詞）

＊S：主詞　V：動詞　O：受詞　C：補語

　IO：間接受詞　DO：直接受詞

2.

(A) The <u>swans</u> are <u>swimming</u>.
         S   V

(B) The <u>swans</u> are <u>following</u> the ducks.
         S   V

(C) <u>They</u> are <u>crossing</u> the <u>river</u>.
   S   V   O

(D) <u>There</u> <u>is</u> an <u>arch bridge</u> across the river.
   S V   SC

延伸參考：

2.

名詞	Swan, duck, wake, flock, banner, reflection, string
動詞	Swim, follow, watch, embed
形容詞或副詞	Small, deeply, in the wake of（接踵）
介系詞	Across, under, over

請聽錄音並覆誦 🎧 ▶Mp3 031

Three swans are swimming across the river.

三隻天鵝正游過這條河。

The swans are following the four ducks ahead of them.

天鵝跟隨牠們前頭的四隻鴨。

The other two ducks are in the wake（航行尾波，可引申為接踵）

of the swans. 其他兩隻鴨子尾隨著天鵝游跡。

There is an arch bridge over the river. 河上有一座拱橋。

Two passers are watching the flocks. 兩個行人在看著禽群。

A string of small banners is under the bridge. 一串小橫幅在橋下。

The lake has a reflection of the vegetation deeply embedding

the whole picture. 湖中有反映了植被深深地嵌入了整個畫面。

3.

3.

A. This is a beach with hot, beautiful, refreshing air.
   S   V   SC

B. Ocean waves lap the sand on the beach.
         S   V   O

C. The breeze is touching every grain of sand.
       S   V   O

D. The sky is idyllic, blue and clear.
       S V   SC

E. The beautiful, big blue ocean's waves are crashing to
                                   S   V

   the cliffs.

延伸參考：

3.

名詞	Beach, air, wave, sand, breeze, grain, sky, cliff
動詞	Lap, touch, crash
形容詞或副詞	hot, beautiful, refreshing, idyllic, blue, clear, beautiful, big blue
介系詞	With, on, of,

請聽錄音並覆誦 🎧 Mp3 031

1. This is a beach with hot, beautiful, refreshing air.

   這是一個熱、美麗、空氣清新的海灘。

2. Ocean waves lap the sand on the beach.

   海浪拍打著海灘上的沙。

3. The breeze is touching every grain of sand.

   微風觸摸著每一粒沙子。

4. The sky is idyllic, blue and clear.

   天空是田園式的、藍的、明亮的。

5. The beautiful, big blue ocean's waves are crashing to the cliffs. 美麗藍海的巨浪沖向懸崖

6. Hot, beautiful, refreshing air drenches heavenly sandy beach. The breeze is touching every grain of sand. The sky is idyllic, blue and clear. The beautiful, big blue ocean's waves are crashing to the cliffs.

   炎熱、美麗、清新的空氣籠罩著天堂般的沙灘。微風撫摸著每一粒沙子。天空是那麼質樸、蔚藍、明亮。藍色大海洋美麗的海浪衝向峭壁。

4.

4.

A. The warm, golden <u>sands</u> <u>run</u> through your toes.
   S **V**

B. The gentle <u>breeze</u> is warmly <u>stroking</u> your <u>face</u>.
   S **V** **O**

C. <u>You</u> <u>sit</u> alone in the bosom of the ocean.
   S **V**

D. <u>You</u> <u>find</u> gorgeous, shiny <u>shells</u> rolling in the waves.
   S **V** **O**

E. The <u>shells</u> have <u>been</u> <u>washed</u> into the shore by the
   S **V** **SC**

   rippling of the water.

延伸參考：

4.

名詞	Sand, toe, breeze, bosom, ocean , shell, shore, rippling
動詞	Run, stroke, sit, find, wash,
形容詞或副詞	warm, golden, gorgeous, shiny
介系詞	Through, in, by

請聽錄音並覆誦 ▶Mp3 031

1. The warm, golden sands run through your toes.

   溫暖的金色沙粒貫穿你的腳趾

2. The gentle breeze is warmly stroking your face.

   柔和的微風溫暖的輕撫你的臉。

3. You sit alone in the bosom of the ocean.

   你獨自一人坐在大海的懷抱中。

4. You find gorgeous, shiny shells rolling in the waves.

   你發現華麗、閃亮的貝殼，在海浪中翻滾。

5. The shells have been washed into the shore by the rippling of the water. 貝殼沖進岸邊水的漣漪之中。

6. The warm, golden sand runs between your toes with the gentle breeze. As you sit alone, you find gorgeous, shiny shells that have been washed into the shore by the rippling of the water.

   溫暖的、金色的沙子在柔和的微風中跑在你的腳趾之間。當你一人獨坐時，你會發現華麗、閃亮的貝殼隨著水的漣漪沖到岸邊。

DAY 4 THURSDAY

1.

1.

A. <u>It</u>'<u>s</u> a cold and sunny <u>day</u>.
 S V   SC

B. <u>They</u>'re <u>looking</u> at a <u>view</u>.
  S   V   O

C. <u>They</u>'re <u>wearing</u> <u>coats</u>.
  S   V   O

D. <u>There</u> <u>is</u> a beautiful <u>reflection</u> in the water.
  S   V   SC

E. The <u>boy</u> <u>has</u> short <u>hair</u>.
      S   V   O

F. The <u>man</u> <u>wears</u> a <u>cap</u>.
      S   V   O

G. The <u>girl</u> <u>has</u> long <u>hair</u>.
      S   V   O

H. The <u>boy</u> <u>wears</u> a sport <u>coat</u>.
      S   V   O

延伸參考：

請聽錄音並覆誦 🎧 **Mp3 032**

1.

It's a cold and sunny day. 這是寒冷而陽光明媚的一天。

They're looking at a view. 他們在看著一片風景。

They're wearing coats. 他們穿著外套。

There is a beautiful reflection in the water. 美麗的倒影在水中。

The boy has short hair. 這個男孩是短頭髮。

The man wears a cap. 那人戴著一頂帽子。

The girl has long hair. 這個女孩是長頭髮。

The boy wears a sport coat. 這個男孩穿運動外套。

It's a cold and sunny day and they're in coats looking at a view. There is a beautiful reflection in the water. The boy has short hair and wears sport coat. The man wears a hat and the girl next to him has long hair.

這是寒冷而陽光明媚的一天，他們穿著外套看著風景，還有美麗的倒影在水中。這個男孩是短髮，穿著運動外套。那人戴著一頂帽子，他身邊的女孩有一頭長髮。

【Day 4】Thursday

2.

2.

A. The <u>cup</u> <u>is</u> <u>in front</u> of the box.
　　　S　V　SC

B. The red <u>beans</u> <u>are</u> <u>filled</u> inside the Dorayaki.
　　　　　S　　V　SC

C. A <u>wallet</u> <u>is</u> <u>behind the box</u>.
　　　S　　V　　SC

D. <u>There</u> <u>are</u> <u>flowers</u> on the cup.
　　　S　　V　　SC

延伸參考：

請聽錄音並覆誦 🎧 Mp3 032

2.

The cup is in front of the box.

這個杯子在盒子前面。

The red beans are filled inside the Dorayaki.

紅豆填滿了銅鑼燒。

A wallet is behind the box.

有個錢包在盒子的後邊。

There are flowers on the cup.

杯子上有花。

There is a box of Dorayaki filled with red beans. A cup with flowers is in front of the box. A wallet is behind the box.

有一整盒填滿紅豆的銅鑼燒。盒子前面有一個綴著花的杯子。錢包在盒子的後邊。

【Day 4】
Thursday

五種單句的基本句型：

1. S+V（主詞＋動詞）
2. S+V+SC（主詞＋動詞＋主詞補語）
3. S+V+O（主詞＋動詞＋受詞）
4. S+V+O+OC（主詞＋動詞＋受詞＋受詞補語）
5. S+V+IO+DO（主詞＋動詞＋間接受詞＋直接受詞）

＊S：主詞　V：動詞　O：受詞　C：補語
　IO：間接受詞　DO：直接受詞

3.

(A) Three <u>rhinos</u> <u>are</u> <u>under the shade</u>.
　　　　S　　V　　SC

(B) The <u>trees</u> <u>are</u> <u>around the rhinos</u>.
　　　S　　V　　SC

(C) <u>They</u> are <u>resting</u> in the yard.
　　S　　　　　V

(D) <u>Two</u> of the rhinos are <u>sleeping</u>.
　　S　　　　　　　　　　　V

　　造句之前，先與同伴腦力激盪一下你們會用到哪些名詞、動詞、形容詞、副詞與介系詞。

延伸參考：

3.

名詞	Rhino, palm tree, rear
動詞	Are, is, rest, sleep
形容詞或副詞	
介系詞	Under, around, behind

請聽錄音並覆誦 🎧 Mp3 032

Three rhinos are under the shade of palm trees.

三隻犀牛在棕櫚樹的樹蔭下。

The weeds are behind the rhinos. 犀牛的背後是雜草。

They are resting in the yard. 他們在院子裡休息。

There is a bunker with iron bars at the rear of the yard.

院子的後面有一個鐵欄杆的碉堡。

Two of the rhinos are sleeping. 其中兩隻犀牛在睡覺。

[Day 4]
Thursday

五種單句的基本句型：

1. S+V（主詞＋動詞）
2. S+V+SC（主詞＋動詞＋主詞補語）
3. S+V+O（主詞＋動詞＋受詞）
4. S+V+O+OC（主詞＋動詞＋受詞＋受詞補語）
5. S+V+IO+DO（主詞＋動詞＋間接受詞＋直接受詞）
＊S：主詞 V：動詞 O：受詞 C：補語
  IO：間接受詞 DO：直接受詞

4.

4.

(A) The <u>bridge</u> <u>connects</u> <u>mountains</u>.
　　　　　S　　　　V　　　　O

(B) The <u>bridge</u> <u>stretches</u> across the stream.
　　　　　S　　　　V

(C) The <u>stream</u> <u>is</u> <u>far below the bridge</u>.
　　　　　S　　V　　　SC

(D) The <u>bridge</u> <u>is</u> <u>in the middle</u> of the valley.
　　　　　S　　　V　　SC

　　造句之前，先與同伴腦力激盪一下你們會用到哪些名詞、動詞、形容詞、副詞與介系詞。

延伸參考：

4.

名詞	Bridge, stream, valley
動詞	Connect, stream
形容詞或副詞	Far, green, shady
介系詞	Across, in, below, forward

請聽錄音並覆誦　🎧 Mp3 032

The bridge connects mountains. 這座橋連接山際。

The bridge stretches across the stream. 這座橋橫跨小溪。

The stream comes down from deep inside of mountains.
小溪從群山深處下來。

The stream passes through the green, shady valley.
溪流穿過綠蔭山谷。

The stream is far below the bridge. 那溪流遠在這座橋下方。

The branches of trees leans forward the center of the stream.
樹的枝枒傾前於溪流的中心。

The bridge is in the middle of the valley. 這座橋位於山谷中間。

【Day 4】
Thursday

五種單句的基本句型：

1. S+V（主詞＋動詞）

2. S+V+SC（主詞＋動詞＋主詞補語）

3. S+V+O（主詞＋動詞＋受詞）

4. S+V+O+OC（主詞＋動詞＋受詞＋受詞補語）

5. S+V+IO+DO（主詞＋動詞＋間接受詞＋直接受詞）

＊S：主詞　V：動詞　O：受詞　C：補語

　　IO：間接受詞　DO：直接受詞

DAY 5 FRIDAY

　　下一章我們就要進入聽力測驗的問答特訓篇了，在那之前我們可以就對於圖的單口敘述延伸為問答的敘述，一方面練習對於看圖問答的敘述能力，一方面也為問答的聽力測驗暖身。

　　以下就回顧的圖片，練習問答，不過我們還是就所說的句子先作五大句型的分析，再延伸圖敘為對話。

1.

1. 甲一問乙一答：

(A) Where is the path leading to?
　　　S 　V 　　SC

(B) Have you been there before?
　　　　S 　V 　SC

(C) What are behind the waterfall?
　　　S 　V 　　　SC

(D) How does it feel like (how) in the waterfall?
　　　　　S 　V 　　SC

乙回答：＿＿＿＿＿＿＿＿＿＿＿＿＿＿＿

延伸參考：

請聽錄音並複誦 🎧 **Mp3 033**

1.

甲問： (A) Where is the path leading to?這條小路通往哪裡？

乙回答： The path leads to the waterfall.這條小路通向瀑布。

甲問： (B) Have you been there before?你去過那裡嗎？

乙回答： Yes, I have been there before.是。我以前去過那裡。

甲問： (C) What are behind the waterfall?瀑布的後面是什麼？

乙回答： A cave is behind the waterfall.
　　　　一個洞穴在瀑布的後面。

甲問： (D) How does it feel like in the waterfall?
　　　　在瀑布裡感覺像甚麼？

乙回答： It feels like in a shower.感覺就像在淋浴。

2.

2. 甲一問乙一答：

(A) What are the trees made of?
      S   V   SC

(B) What are the trunks bound/tied with?
      S   V   SC

(C) What do you think the trees are for?
      O   S   V

(D) What are behind the trees?
      S   V   SC

乙回答：_____

延伸參考：

請聽錄音並複誦 🎧 Mp3 033

2.

> 甲問： (A) What are the trees made of?樹是什麼做的？
>
> 乙回答： The trees are made of bamboo.樹由竹子製成。
>
> 甲問： (B) What are the trunks bound with?
>
> > 樹幹上綁著什麼？
>
> 乙回答： The trunks are bound with barrier tape.
>
> > 樹木被隔離帶綁著。
>
> 甲問： (C) What do you think the trees are for?
>
> > 你認為那些樹是什麼用途？
>
> 乙回答： I think the trees are a sign for gingko trees.
>
> > 我認為那樹是銀杏樹的標誌。
>
> 甲問： (D) What are behind the trees?樹後面是什麼？
>
> 乙回答： There are gingko trees behind the sign.
>
> > 標誌背後是銀杏樹。

【Day 5】
Friday

3.

3. 甲一問乙一答：

(A) Where is the playground?
   S   V   SC

(B) Where are the ladders leading to?
   S   V   SC

(C) Have you played with the swings?
        S   V

(D) Why isn't there anybody?
      V   S   SC

乙回答：＿＿＿＿＿＿＿＿＿＿＿

延伸參考：

請聽錄音並複誦 🎧 **Mp3 033**

3.　甲問：　(A) Where is the playground?

遊樂場在哪裡？

　　乙回答：　The playground is in the woods.

遊樂場在樹林裡。

　　甲問：　(B) Where are the ladders leading to?

階梯通往哪裡？

　　乙回答：　The ladders lead to the woods.

階梯進入樹林裡。

　　甲問：　(C) Have you played with the swings?

你玩過那些鞦韆嗎？

　　乙回答：　Yes. I have played with the swings.

是。我玩過那些鞦韆。

　　甲問：　(D) Why isn't there anybody?

為什麼都沒有任何人？

　　乙回答：　Because it is going to rain.

因為要下雨了。

【Day 5】Friday

4.

4. 甲一問乙一答：

(A) <u>What</u> is the <u>stilt walker</u> <u>doing</u> to the crowds?
　　O　　　　　S　　　　V

(B) <u>What</u> is the <u>stilt walker</u> <u>holding</u>?
　　O　　　　　S　　　　V

(C) <u>What</u> is the <u>woman</u> <u>doing</u> to him?
　　O　　　　　S　　　V

(D) How are the <u>crowds</u> <u>reacting</u>?
　　　　　　　　S　　　V

乙回答：＿＿＿＿＿＿＿＿＿＿＿＿＿＿＿＿＿

延伸參考：

請聽錄音並複誦 🎧 **Mp3 033**

4.　**甲問**：(A) What is the stilt walker doing to the crowds?

　　　　　　高蹺人正向人群幹什麼？

　乙回答：The stilt walker is performing to the crowds.

　　　　　　高蹺人正表演給群眾看。

　　甲問：(B) What is the stilt walker holding?

　　　　　　高蹺人拿著什麼？

　乙回答：The stilt walker is holding an umbrella.

　　　　　　高蹺人撐著傘。

　　甲問：(C) What is the woman doing to him?

　　　　　　那個女人正在對他做什麼？

　乙回答：The woman is taking a picture of him.

　　　　　　那女人正在拍他的照片。

　　甲問：(D) How are the crowds reacting?

　　　　　　群眾如何反應？

　乙回答：The crowds are paying attention on him.

　　　　　　群眾關注他的表演。

WEEK 4

問答特訓篇

WEEK 4 問答特訓篇

DAY 1 MONDAY

多益的問答考法與全民英檢不同的是，它的問題與答案是完全看不見的，只能以聽來作答，問答測驗是第二部分，從第 11 至第 40 共 30 題都是一樣的文字：

Mark your answer on your answer sheet（在答案卷上填答）

我們先模擬十題，然後再就測驗內容延伸對話。

請打開音檔：🎧 Mp3 034

1-10 Mark your answer on your answer sheet.

核對答案：

1.C 2. A 3. B 4.A 5.A 6.B 7.C 8.A 9.B 10.A

一般人做完聽力模擬測驗，核對過答案，就好像沒事了，就像學校裡司空見慣煩不勝煩的小考、段考，考完了鬆口氣就丟到腦後去了。這樣看待這個練習，你的聽力自然是不會進步的。我們應該把剛才考過的資料，好好的利用來發揮在實際生活中的經驗，繼續把話題延伸下去，讓你與你的同伴在聽完母語人士的聲音以後，能夠有機會模仿它們，而繼續把那個情境內化進自己的語境之中，才會深刻體驗這段聽力測驗的實用性。所以接下來請同學甲再播放一次 1-10 題，然後複誦題句，再由同學乙回答正確答案。然後再由乙同學針對甲所問的話題反問甲，或延伸甲的話題，再聊一些別的事，讓互動衍生出來，不再限於先前單調的測驗。

　　每題播放前先參照一下它的問答的情境，如：Greeting 問候語、Asking Information 問詢、Making Suggestions 提議、Making Phonecalls 電話用語、Agreement 同意與肯定、On the Menu 用餐、Subjects in the College 大學學科、Wear 服裝、Guess and Certainty 猜測與事實、Asking for Favors 請求協助等等小的情境。也有些是較的大情境，如：Association 社交、Phone-calling 電話、In the Office 辦公室用語、School 學校、Household 居家、Daily Life 日常生活、Figures 人物、Shopping 購物、Foods 食物、Dining 用餐、Health 健康、Nature 大自然、Traveling 旅遊、Leisure Time 休閒娛樂、Media 媒體、Social Issues 社會議題等等。先有進入該情境的準備，就比較容易創造出適宜的對話。

　　其次，問答的聽力基本技巧就是注意所問是 Yes/No 還是 Wh-類的問題。如果他是以 Be 動詞或其他助動詞引導的問題，就必然是 Yes/No 類的問題，須以 Be 動詞或該助動詞回答。如果他是以 Wh-疑問詞引導的問題，就必然是 Wh- 類的問題，須以該相關疑問詞回答。舉例如下：

Yes/no 問句	
Be 動詞問句	回答參考
Are you a student?	Yes, I **am** a student.
Was he a teacher?	No, he **was** not a teacher.
Were they all Chinese?	Yes, they **were** all Chinese.
Is this mine?	No, this **is** not yours.

助動詞問句	回答參考
Can she sing?	Yes, she **can** sing.
Will I see you tomorrow?	No, you **will** not see me tomorrow.
Has he eaten?	Yes, he **has**.
Did he stay?	No, he **didn't**.
Would you fax it to me?	Of course I **would**.
Could she be the winner?	No, she **couldn't**.
Should we go now?	Certainly.
Wh- 問句 （此類問題最重要的是要聽清楚其開頭的第一個 wh- 字）	
What 問什麼	回答參考
What is your favorite color?	My favorite color is blue.
Where 問地點	回答參考
Where am I?	You are in Taiwan.
When 問時間	回答參考
When is the museum open?	It is open at 8 a.m.
Why 問理由	回答參考
Why is he late?	He missed the bus.
Who 問誰	回答參考
Who is he?	He is my father.
How 問如何	回答參考
How are you?	I am fine. Thank you.

再就剛才的測驗內容延伸對話。 **Mp3 035**

Asking for Favors 請求協助

1. **播放** Would you mind typing in this letter/report, please?
   暫停

   甲複誦 Would you mind typing in this letter/report, please?
   麻煩幫我打字這封信/報告好嗎？

   乙回答 No, not at all.（沒問題。）

   反問 _____

   甲回答 _____

Asking Information 問詢

2. **播放** How long have you been living here? **暫停**

   甲複誦 How long have you been living here?
   你在這裡住了多久？

   乙回答 Since 2001.（自2001年至今。）

   反問 _____

   甲回答 _____

Asking Information 問詢

3. **播放** What does he look like? **暫停**

   甲複誦 What does he look like?
   他像是幹哪一行的？

   乙回答 A doctor or a lawyer.（一個醫生或律師。）

   反問 _____

   甲回答 _____

Making Suggestions 提議

4.   **播放** How about going to the movie?

      暫停

   甲複誦 How about going to the movie? 一起去看電影如何？

   乙回答 Good idea! （好主意！）

    反問 _____

   甲回答 _____

---

1. 相關情境

請求幫忙的說法

問句	肯定句
Could you do me a favor? Can I ask a favor of you? Will you do me a favor? Can you give me a hand with this letter? Will you do something for me?	I wonder if you do me a favor. I have a favor to ask you. If you don't mind, I need you to type this letter for me.

答應幫忙的說法	乙反問	甲回答
No problem, I'll do it. Sure, if I can. Sure, I'll help you. Yes, of course.	When will you need it? 你甚麼時候要？	The sooner the better. 越快越好。

2. 相關情境

乙反問	甲回答
And you? 你呢？	I just moved in. 我剛搬來？
How long have you been studying here? 你在這裡讀多久了？	Two years. 兩年了。
How long have you been working here? 你在這工作多久了？	A decade. 十年了。

3. 相關情境

乙反問	甲回答
Why do you want to know? 你為甚麼想知道？	I just wonder at my professor's look. 我只是想知道我的教授的長相。
Why do you ask? 為甚麼要問？	I'm going to pick him up at the airport. 我要去機場接他。 （還不認識）
Why? 甚麼事？	Everybody knows him except me. 除了我大家都認識他了。

4. 相關情境		
乙反問		甲回答
Which theater do you prefer? 你喜歡哪家戲院？		How about Broadway? 百老匯戲院如何？
Which movie are we going to see? 我們要看哪部電影？		Do you like Transformers? 你喜歡「變形金剛」嗎？
Are there any others coming with us? 還有誰要一起去看？		Just two of us. 就我們兩人。

Ordering Food 點餐

5.　　　播放 Could I have a look at the menu, please? 暫停

　　甲複誦 Could I have a look at the menu, please?

　　　　　（我可以看看菜單嗎？）

　　乙回答 OK. Here you are.（沒問題，拿去。）

　　　反問 _____

　　甲回答 _____

Traveling 旅遊

6.　　　播放 Do you have any luggage, sir? 暫停

　　甲複誦 Do you have any luggage, sir?

　　　　　（您攜帶了行李嗎？）

　　乙回答 Just this one suitcase.（就是這件手提箱。）

　　　反問 _____

　　甲回答 _____

Phone-calling in the Office 辦公室電話用語

7.　　播放 I'd like to speak to the manager, please. 暫停

　　　甲複誦 I'd like to speak to the manager, please.

　　　　　　（我想找經理談。）

　　　乙回答 I'm sorry. She's not here.

　　　　　　（抱歉！她不在這裡。）

　　　反問 ＿＿＿＿＿＿＿＿＿＿＿＿＿＿＿＿＿＿＿＿

　　　甲回答 ＿＿＿＿＿＿＿＿＿＿＿＿＿＿＿＿＿＿＿＿

Recreation娛樂

8.　　播放 I like soccer game seasons. 暫停

　　　甲複誦 I like soccer game seasons.

　　　　　　（我喜歡足球季。）

　　　乙回答 So do I.（我也是。）

　　　反問 ＿＿＿＿＿＿＿＿＿＿＿＿＿＿＿＿＿＿＿＿

　　　甲回答 ＿＿＿＿＿＿＿＿＿＿＿＿＿＿＿＿＿＿＿＿

Transportation 交通

9.　　播放 May I see your driving license, please? 暫停

　　　甲複誦 May I see your driving license, please?

　　　　　　（我可以看看你的駕照嗎？）

　　　乙回答 Of course.（當然可以。）

　　　反問 ＿＿＿＿＿＿＿＿＿＿＿＿＿＿＿＿＿＿＿＿

　　　甲回答 ＿＿＿＿＿＿＿＿＿＿＿＿＿＿＿＿＿＿＿＿

In the Office 辦公室用語

10.   播放 Could I speak to Mr. Snow, please? 暫停

    甲複誦 Could I speak to Mr. Snow, please?

      （我可以找史諾先生嗎？）

    乙回答 I'll put you through to his secretary now, sir.

      （先生，我幫你轉接給他的秘書。）

    甲回答 _____

---

5. 相關情境

乙反問	甲回答
Anything else? 還需要甚麼嗎？	Bring me some water, please. 請給我一些水。
What else would you like? 還需要甚麼嗎？	I will tell you later. 稍後我再告訴你。
Is that all? 就這些嗎？	That's it. Thanks. 就這樣了，謝謝。

---

6. 相關情境

乙反問	甲回答
What is the baggage allowance? 行李限額是多少？	It is 20 kilos for the economy class. 經濟艙 20 公斤。
Is it overweight? 過重了嗎？	Oh, it is overweight. 喔！過重了。
How much does it cost for excess baggage? 超重費用是多少？	It is NT$ 1000. 台幣一千元。

7. 相關情境

乙反問	甲回答
Would you like to leave a massage? 你要留言嗎？	No, that's OK. I'll call back later. 不必了，沒關係，我稍後再打來。
Do you want to leave a massage? 你要留言嗎？	No, that's OK. I'll call again. 不必了，沒關係，我稍後再打來。
May I take a message? 需要我幫你留話嗎？	Yes, my number is 12345678. 好的，我的電話號碼是 12345678。

8. 相關情境

乙反問	甲回答
What's your favorite team? 你最愛哪隊？	Liverpool. 利物浦隊。
Who will most possibly be the champion this year? 今年哪隊最可能得冠軍？	Manchester United. 曼徹斯特聯隊。
Where do you like to catch the game? 你喜歡在哪看球賽？	On TV. 看電視。

9. 相關情境

乙反問	甲回答
What can I do for you, officer? 我能效勞嗎，警官？	You just made an illegal turn. 你剛才違規轉彎了。
Anything wrong, officer? 我做錯甚麼了嗎？	Just an ordinary spot check. 就是例行臨檢。
Is there something wrong? 出了甚麼問題嗎？	You didn't wear your seat belt. 你未繫安全帶。

10. 相關情境

甲回答：Thanks for help. 謝謝幫忙。

要找的人不在時的說法

No, he is out. 他出去了。	No, he is not around. 他不在附近。
No, he is not available. 他不在。	He just stepped out. 他剛走出去。

對照上一回的多益模擬題，請大家試做模擬全民英檢的問答測驗。

請播音檔。　Mp3 036

1. A. Just fine, thanks.

   B. So am I.

   C. They're doing home.

   D. No, I do nothing.

2. A. Some fruits.

   B. Every morning.

   C. Two months ago.

   D. In Taipei.

3. A. Well, he's out now.

   B. Sorry, I'm busy tonight.

   C. Sure, I'll make it up.

   D. Yeah, I think it's a good story.

4. A. In the next door.

   B. Right after the movie.

   C. About the story.

   D. Her boyfriend, I think.

5. A. It's close to the bus stop.

   B. There's a museum near here.

   C. Usually at 5, except for Sunday.

   D. It's open every day.

6. A. Yes, I went there last year.

   B. Yes, I've seen it once.

   C. No, I don't know where it is.

   D. No, I wasn't there.

7. A. No. Mary is on another line.

   B. Sure, I'll be in my office until 5.

   C. All right. Call it off.

   D. Yes, please.

8. A. That's a good news.

   B. But I like this one better.

   C. Oh, I'm glad he's better.

   D. Yeah, I've asked his mother.

9. A. I'll move to the line.

   B. Really? Where is the line?

   C. I'm sorry. I'll put it on your desk tomorrow.

   D. I won't cross the line.

10. A. She starts tomorrow.

    B. I like her idea, too.

    C. She is idle today.

    D. Neither do I.

11. A. Yes, you may be excused.

    B. Yes, there's one on the next corner.

    C. Yes, it belongs to my neighbors.

    D. Yes, this is Park Road.

12. A. I'd like to stay.

    B. I'm going to take it.

    C. I love to play football.

    D. Medium, please.

13. A. Yes, I'll give him a tour of the college.

    B. No, I want to be an English major.

    C. No, I went to college in Taiwan.

    D. Yes, most of my friends joined a club.

14. A. Yes, you could try this room.

    B. Well, the color is too dark.

    C. No, there're no mice.

    D. Certainly. One moment, please.

15. A. Sorry, I don't have a ticket.

    B. You got 70 tickets, remember?

    C. Didn't you put it in your pocket?

    D. Sure, I'll tick it on the form.

【Day 2】Tuesday

核對答案：

1.A 2.D 3.B 4.D 5.A 6.A 7.B 8.C 9.C 10.D

11.B 12.D 13.B 14.D 15.C

上一節我們提到過 Yes/No 問句與 Wh 問句的應答要領，這一節我們就進一步介紹基本的 Yes/No 問句的句尾揚音，以及肯定句的下降音，隨著母語人士的讀音，練習音調再次熟習問答聽力測驗的技巧。

開始播放音檔並複誦，每播放一句問答停頓八秒鐘 Mp3 037

Activity One

A. Be 動詞 (am, are, is, was, were)

語調：

問：Am I late?

答：Yes, you are. 或 No, you are not.

語調：

問：Are you a student?

答：Yes, I am. 或 No, I am not.

語調：

問：Is he on vacation?

答：Yes, he is. 或 No, he isn't.

語調：

問：Was he your teacher?

答：Yes, he was. 或 No, he wasn't.

語調：

問：Were you scared?

答：Yes, I was. 或 No, I wasn't.

B. 助動詞 (do, does, did, can, may, will, should, would, could, might, have, has)

語調：

問：Do you like watching TV?

答：Yes, I do. 或 No, I don't.

語調：

問：Does she smoke?

答：Yes, she does. 或 No, she doesn't.

語調：

問：Did you do the dish?

答：Yes, I did. 或 No, I didn't.

語調：

問：Can you ride the bicycle?

答：Yes, I can. 或 No, I can't.

語調：

問：May I come to visit you?

答：Yes, you may. 或 No, you may not.

語調：

問：Will you buy the car?

答：Yes, I will. 或 No, I won't.

語調：

問：Should I give her some money?

答：Yes, you should. 或 No, you shouldn't.

語調：

問：Would you be quiet?

答：Yes, I would. 或 No, I wouldn't.

語調：

問：Might I see him just once more?

答：Yes, you might. 或 No, you might never see him again.

語調：

問：Have you cleaned the floor?

答：Yes, I have. 或 No, I haven't

語調：

問：Has he made the promise?

答：Yes, he has. 或 No, he hasn't.

接下來，再把剛才的測驗內容延伸問答練習，請播放音檔。 Mp3 038

Activity Two

Greeting問候語

　　播放1. How are you doing? 暫停

　　甲複誦 How are you doing?（一切都好嗎？）

　乙回答： Just fine, thanks.（都還好，謝謝！）

　　反問： And you?（你呢?）

　甲回答：＿＿＿＿＿＿＿＿＿＿＿＿＿＿＿＿＿

　　　　　（接著可以自由的多談一些問候的話）

Asking Information問詢

    播放2. Where did you live?

     暫停

    甲複誦 Where did you live?（你過去住哪兒？）

    乙回答： In Taipei.（在台北。）

    反問： And you?（你呢？）

    甲回答： _____

Making Suggestions 提議

    播放3. Let's go to see a movie tonight.

     暫停

    甲複誦 Let's go to see a movie tonight.

        （今晚一道看電影吧！）

    乙回答： Sorry, I'm busy tonight.（抱歉！今晚我很忙。）

    甲提議： _____

Asking Information問詢

    播放4. Who's Jennifer watching now?

     暫停

    甲複誦 Who's Jennifer watching now?（珍妮佛正盯著誰看？）

    乙回答： Her boyfriend, I think.（我想可能是她男友。）

    反問： Why do you ask?（幹嘛問？）

    甲回答： _____

1. 相關情境

問候語的說法

問候	回應
How are you?	I'm fine. /Just fine.
How have you been?	Good. /Pretty good.
How are you doing?	OK.
How's it going?	Not too bad.
What's up?	Nothing.
What's new?	Not much.
Long time no see.	Yeah, it's been a while.

2. 相關情境

問詢住處的說法

Where do you live? 住哪裡？	I live in the school dormitory.（宿舍）
	I live in Taoyuan City.
	I live in the suburbs.（市郊）
Whom do you live with ? 與誰同住？	I live with my classmate.（同學）
	I live with my roommate.（室友）
	I live with my family.（家人）

3. 相關情境

各種提議

I know you're busy preparing your test tomorrow, but this movie is just for your test.

我知道你忙著明天的考試，但這部片子正是你考試所需要的。

I know you have to work overtime, but this is the boss's invitation.

我知道你必須加班，但這次是老闆請你看電影。

Maybe some other time. I found a movie just suit for you.

或許下次吧！我知道一部適合你的電影。

4. 相關情境

聊八卦

She's been staring at him during class for a week.

她這個禮拜上課時都在盯他。

I think she is always wandering at office hours.

我覺得她上班時總是心不在焉 / 放空。

Don't you think she looked like having a crush on the guy?

你不覺得她像是喜歡上那傢伙了？

Asking Information問詢

播放5. I heard John made it better today. **暫停**

甲複誦： I heard John made it better today.
（聽說約翰今天做得好多了。）

乙回答： Oh, that's a good news.（那真是好消息。）

反問： I still don't know what's wrong with him. Do you know?（我還是搞不清楚他有甚麼問題，你知道嗎？）

甲回答： ＿＿＿＿＿＿＿＿＿＿＿＿＿＿＿＿＿＿＿＿＿＿

【Day 2】
Tuesday

Asking Information問詢

播放6. Have you ever been to Mountain Ali before? **暫停**

甲複誦： Have you ever been to Mountain Ali before?
（你去過阿里山嗎？）

乙回答： Yes, I went there last year.（有，我去年去過。）

反問： Have you?（你呢？）

甲回答： ＿＿＿＿＿＿＿＿＿＿＿＿＿＿＿＿＿＿＿＿＿＿

乙再問： Oh Really? How was that?（喔，是嗎？感覺如何？）

甲再答： ＿＿＿＿＿＿＿＿＿＿＿＿＿＿＿＿＿＿＿＿＿＿

Making Phone Calls電話用語

播放7. Sorry, I've got to run now. May I call you back tonight? **暫停**

甲複誦： Sorry, I've got to run now. May I call you back later?
（抱歉！我必須先走，現在得先掛電話了，可以今晚再打給你嗎？）

乙回答： Sure, I'll be in my office until 5.

（沒問題，5點以前我都在辦公室。）

反問： What's so hurry?（忙甚麼？）

甲回答：_____

Asking Information問詢

播放8. When does the museum open on weekdays? **暫停**

甲複誦 When does the museum open on weekdays?

（博物館平日幾點開放？）

乙回答： It's usually at 5, except for Sunday.

（除週日外，都是五點。）

反問： Is there something interests you?

（展覽有甚麼吸引你的嗎？）

甲回答：_____

乙提醒： Mind you! Don't sneak out for it at office hours. The boss has an eye on you.

（當心喔！別在上班時溜出去，老闆正盯著你。）

Advice and Suggestion 勸告與建議

播放9. You are two days behind on your deadline. **暫停**

甲複誦 You are two days behind on your deadline.

（你的作業已經超過期限兩天了。）

乙回答： I'm sorry. I'll put it on your desk tomorrow.

（抱歉！我明天會放在你桌上的。）

甲回答：_____

5. 相關情境

They said he didn't work hard enough lately.
聽説他最近不怎麼用功。

I'm not so sure, either. Something like getting too nervous I guess.
我也不清楚，我猜大概是太緊張吧！

Well it's the depression, everybody has a hard time.
唉！不景氣嘛！大家都不好過。

6. 相關情境

No, but I've just finished a trip with Sun Moon Lake Bike Trail which has recently been named one of the World's top 10 biking trails.
我沒去過，但剛剛參加了日月潭單車之旅，該活動最近榮登世界前十大單車之旅。

The mesmerizing Sun Moon Lake Bike Trail offers romantic lake side views and rich ecosystems.
迷人的日月潭單車之旅可以讓你享受浪漫的湖畔景致以及豐富的生態風光。

7. 相關情境

The bell just rang; I'm already late for the class!
上課鐘剛響，我已經遲到了！

My meeting is about to begin, and I haven't set everything up!
快開會了，我甚麼都還沒準備好哩！

It's Mary. Her water is broken, and I need to send her to the hospital immediately.
是瑪麗啦！她的羊水剛破了，我得趕快送她去醫院了。

8. 相關情境

Nothing, just the homework of my history class.
沒甚麼，就是歷史課作業而已。

I have to arrange the itinerary of my client's visit.
我必須安排客戶來訪的行程。

It's the Painting Anime. They made a great animation imitating paintings so alive. 是古畫動漫，博物館模古畫模擬得非常生動。

9. 相關情境

You better be, or you will be flunked this term!
最好如此，不然你這學期就要被當掉了。

You had better turn it in tonight. The whole project is delayed by it.
你最好今晚交件，整個企劃案都讓你耽擱了。

Hurry up! The community needs the plan to prepare the party.
快點！社區正等著計畫準備聚會。

Agreement 同意與肯定

10.   播放 Honestly, I don't think Jenny's idea will work. **暫停**

    甲複誦 Honestly, I don't think Jenny's idea will work.

        （坦白說，我不認為珍妮的想法有用。）

  乙回答： Neither do I.（我也是。）

  反問： What about the professor's / boss's /others' opinion?（教授/老闆/其他人怎麼想？）

  甲回答： _____

【Day 2】Tuesday

Asking Information 問詢

11.   播放 Excuse me, is there a parking lot in this neighborhood? **暫停**

    甲複誦 Excuse me, is there a parking lot in this neighborhood?

        （耽誤您一下，請問附近有停車場嗎？）

  乙回答： Yes, there's one on the next corner.

        （有，在下一個轉角處。）

  甲再問： How do I get there?（該怎麼走？）

  乙回答： _____

On the Menu 用餐

12.   播放 How would you like your steak? **暫停**

    甲複誦 How would you like your steak?

        （您的牛排要幾分熟？）

  乙回答： Medium, please.（請給我五分熟。）

  甲問： Would you pass me the salt shaker?

        （請把鹽罐遞給我。）

10. 相關情境

同意與肯定

The professor told me the project can't be funded.
教授說這個計畫得不到經費。

I don't know yet, but I think the boss will agree with us.
我還不知道，不過我想老闆會同意我們的意見。

I can go for Jenny, but others don't think so.
我可以贊成珍妮，但其他人不這麼想。

11. 相關情境

問路的說法

Where is the Park Road?	公園路在哪？
Which way leads to Park Road?	走哪條路可到公園路？
Could you tell me the way to Park Road?	可否請問走哪條路可到公園路？
How can I get to Park Road?	往公園路怎麼走？

回答方向的說法

It's over there.	就在那裡。
It's on this street.	就在這條街上。
It's on the (right / left) corner.	在右邊／左邊轉角。
It's on the right / left-hand side of the street.	在這條路的右／左邊。
It's the third store from the corner.	轉角數過去第三家店。
It's on the opposite side of the street.	在街對面。
It's across from the street.	在街對面。
It's kitty-corner from the store.	在那家店的斜對面。
It's diagonal to the store.	在那家店的斜對面。
Go straight / right / left. It's straight ahead.	直／右／左走。往前直走就是。
Turn right/left. Take a right / left turn.	左／右轉。

12. 相關情境

牛排的熟度		餐桌上所需的調味料及用具	
Raw	全生	Ginger	薑
Rare	三分	Garlic	蒜
Medium Rare	五分	Chili	辣椒
Medium Well	八分	Curry	咖哩
Well done	全熟	Toothpicks	牙籤
		Salt shaker	鹽罐
		Corkscrew	開瓶器

【Day 2】
Tuesday

Subjects in the College 大學學科

13.　　播放 Do you plan to major in History in college?

　　暫停

　甲複誦 Do you plan to major in History in college?

　　　　（你計畫大學要主修歷史嗎？）

　乙回答： No, I want to be an English major.

　　　　（不，我想主修英文。）

　反問： How about you?（你呢？）

甲回答： _____

Wear服裝

14.　　**播放** This coat is a bit tight. Could I try on a larger size?

　　暫停

　　甲複誦 This coat is a bit tight. Could I try on a larger size?

　　　　（這件襯衫太緊了，有大一號的嗎？）

　　乙回答： Certainly. Just a moment, please.（沒問題，馬上來）

　　反問： Here you go, a larger size. Is that fit?

　　　　（大一號的來了，合身嗎？）

　　甲回答： ＿＿＿＿＿＿＿＿＿＿＿＿＿＿＿＿＿＿＿

Guess and Certainty 猜測與事實

15.　　**播放** Oh, my goodness! I just can't remember where I put my ticket.

　　暫停

　　甲複誦 Oh, my goodness! I just can't remember where I put my ticket.（天哪！我就是記不得票放哪了。）

　　乙反問： Didn't you put it in your pocket?

　　　　（你不是放口袋了嗎？）

　　甲回答： ＿＿＿＿＿＿＿＿＿＿＿＿＿＿＿＿＿＿＿

13. 相關情境

大學各種學科略舉

會計 Accounting	農業系 Agriculture
農業經濟 Agricultural Economics	農業化工 Agricultural Chemistry
畜牧 Animal Husbandry	人類學 Anthropology
應用數學 Applied Mathematics	金融 Banking
生物化學 Biochemistry	植物學 Botany
土木工程 Civil Engineering	控制工程 Control Engineering
電腦資訊 Computer Information	舞蹈 Dance
營養學系 Dietetics	環境工程 Environmental Engineering
水產學 Fishery Technology	食品學 Food Science
外語 Foreign Language	森林 Forestry
地理 Geography	歷史 History

園藝 Horticulture	國際貿易關係學 International Relations
國際貿易系 Dept. of Interational Trade	昆蟲 Entomology
電子工程 Electronic Engineering	電機工程 Electrical Engineering
物理 Physics	哲學 Philosophy
衛生工程學 Sanitary Engineering	戲劇 Theatricals
體育系 Physical Culture	工業管理 Industrial Management
新聞學 Journalism	法律 Law
機械工程 Mechancial Engineering	大眾傳播 Mass Communication
海洋科學 Nautical Science	政治學 Political Science
外交 Diplomacy	經濟 Economic

14. 相關情境

Yes, but I found it doesn't suit me. 合身，但我發現不合適。

Yes, it fits. I'll take this one. 合身，這件我要了。

Yes, now it matches my pants. 合身，現在就可搭配我的褲子了。

15. 相關情境

I probably left it in the classroom. 我可能遺忘在教室裡了。

Let me see. Ah! It's here. 我看看，在這裡。

No, it's not in the pocket. I guess it is in the car.
不，不在口袋，我猜是在車上。

　　以上所延伸的對話只是拋磚引玉的相關情境，相信躍躍欲試的同學一定很想多聊一聊自己的想法，那就盡情的發揮吧！

　　或許有些人就只能說這樣一問一答的話，多了就算想說也「愛說在心口難開」。沒關係！最少你可以從一問一答發展為兩問兩答了，稍後就自然可以發展出進一步的對話，藉著後面「簡短對話」的模擬測驗再去發展自己的簡短對話。

DAY ③ WEDNESDAY

我們再模擬十題多益問答聽力測驗，然後再就測驗內容延伸對話。

請打開音檔： 🔊 Mp3 039

1-10 Mark your answer on your answer sheet.

核對答案：

1.B　2.C　3.B　4.A　5.C　6.A　7.C　8.B　9.B　10.C

再播放剛才的測驗內容以延伸對話。 🔊 Mp3 040

Asking Information and Expression of Time
時間的詢問與表達

1.　　播放 What time do you get to work every day?　暫停

　　甲複誦 What time do you get to work every day?

　　　　（你每天幾點上班？）

　　乙回答 Earlier than 8:30.（八點半之前。）

　　反問 _____

　　甲回答 _____

Working/School Hours 上下班/學

2.　　播放 Is he back from work/school yet?　暫停

　　甲複誦 Is he back from work/school yet?

　　　　（他下班/放學了嗎？）

　　乙回答 Not yet.（還沒。）

　　反問 _____

　　甲回答 _____

Asking Favor at Office 辦公室求助

3.　　播放 Where should I get the files?　暫停

　　甲複誦 Where should I get the files?

　　　　　（我該在哪找檔案？）

　　乙回答 Ask the secretary.（問秘書。）

　　　反問 _____

　　甲回答 _____

Advices and Suggestions 勸告與建議

4.　　播放 I've got a problem.　暫停

　　甲複誦 I've got a problem.（我有一些麻煩。）

　　　乙問 What is it?（甚麼麻煩？）

　　甲回答 _____

---

1. 相關情境

反問：And you? 你呢？

甲回答：About 9 a.m. 九點左右。

詢問時間的說法

What time is it now? 現在幾時？

Can you tell me what time is it? 請問現在幾時？

What time do you have? 你知道現在幾時？

What's the time, please? 請問現在幾時？

---

2. 相關情境

反問：Do you want to see him? 你要找他嗎？

甲回答：Yes, something about the homework/business。
是的，有關家庭作業 / 公事。

加班 / 下班休息的說法

Are you working late this evening? 你今晚工作到很晚嗎？
Are you working overtime tonight? 你今晚加班嗎？
Let's finish up. 我們工作告一段落吧！
Let's call it a day! 今天就到這裡吧！
Let's go home! 我們回家吧！

3. 相關情境

反問：What kind of files are you looking for?
你找的是哪類檔案？

甲回答：It's the annual work plan, and I need to copy them.
我找年度工作計畫，而且要影印。

請人幫忙影印的說法

Could photocopy this report/material for me?
請你幫我影印這份報告 / 資料好嗎？

Do you have time to help me photocopy these papers?
你有空幫我影印這些文件嗎？

I'd appreciate it if you could help me photocopy these documents.
若你能幫我影印這些公文就太感謝了。

> **4. 相關情境**
>
> The copy machine doesn't work. 影印機壞了。
>
> The copy machine isn't working. 影印機壞了。
>
> The copier is broken. 影印機壞了。
>
> I think it ran out of paper. 我想它沒紙了。

Pastime and Hobbies 休閒嗜好

5.　　　　播放 Do you watch the TV news every day?　暫停

　　甲複誦 Do you watch the TV news every day?

　　　　（你每天看電視新聞嗎？）

　　乙回答 Yes, I do.（是的。）

　　反問 _____

　　甲回答 _____

（再延伸）甲：_____

　　　　乙：_____

Pastime and Hobbies 休閒嗜好

6.　　　　播放 What do you think of this painting?　暫停

　　甲複誦 What do you think of this painting?

　　　　（你覺得那幅畫如何？）

　　乙回答 The first one or the second one?

　　　　（第一幅還是第二幅？）

　　甲回答 _____

（再延伸）甲：_____

　　　　乙：_____

Phone-calling 打電話

7.　　　　播放 I am afraid you have the wrong phone number.

　　　　暫停

　　　甲複誦 I am afraid you have the wrong phone number.
　　　　　　（恐怕你撥錯號碼了。）

　　　乙回答 Oh, I'm sorry.（喔，抱歉！）

　　　　反問　_____

　　　甲回答　_____

（再延伸）甲：　_____

　　　　乙：　_____

---

5. 相關情境

反問：What do you do at your pastime except watching TV news?
　　　除了看電視新聞你還用甚麼打發時間？

甲回答：I like surfing the web. 我喜歡上網。

聊休閒嗜好

問：	答：
What do you do after class/school? 你下課 / 放學後做甚麼？ What do you do when you're free? 你休閒時做甚麼？ 或 What are you interested in? 你喜歡甚麼活動？	I like to play games/sports. 我喜歡玩遊戲 / 運動。 或 I like to go shopping/fishing/swimming/painting. 我喜歡去逛街購物 / 釣魚 / 游泳 / 繪畫。

6. 相關情境

甲回答：The one with my son's signature. Isn't he a talent?
那幅有我兒子簽名的畫。你看他是不是天才？

What can we learn form a painting class? 在繪畫班可以學到甚麼？	We can discuss works of art incorporating proper vocabulary. 我們可以結合適當的詞彙來討論的藝術作品。 We can learn about different artists and their style of life. 我們可以瞭解不同的藝術家和他們的生活風格。 We can express creativity. 我們可以表達創意。

【Day 3】
Wednesday

7. 相關情境

反問：What number are you calling? 你撥打了什麼號碼？

甲回答：5553456, I found it on the website.
5553456，我在網站上找到的。

打錯電話的問答

Sorry, you have the wrong number. 抱歉，你打錯號碼了。 Sorry. There is no one here by the name. 抱歉，這裡沒有叫這個名字的人。 Sorry. There is no one named Johnnie here. 抱歉，這裡沒有叫 Johnnie 的這個人。	Oh, sorry, I dialed the wrong number. 喔！抱歉！我打錯號碼了。

Asking Direction 問路

8.　　　　播放 Can you tell me which way south is?　暫停

　　　　甲複誦 Can you tell me which way south is?

　　　　　　（可否告訴我南方是哪邊？）

　　　　乙回答 It's that way.（那邊。）

　　　　反問 ＿＿＿＿＿＿＿＿＿＿＿＿＿＿＿＿＿

　　　　甲回答 ＿＿＿＿＿＿＿＿＿＿＿＿＿＿＿＿＿

（再延伸）乙：＿＿＿＿＿＿＿＿＿＿＿＿＿＿＿＿＿

　　　　甲：＿＿＿＿＿＿＿＿＿＿＿＿＿＿＿＿＿

Promise 承諾

9.　　　　播放 You can't have my laptop. You'll lose it.　暫停

　　　　甲複誦 You can't have my laptop. You'll lose it.

　　　　　　（你不能拿我的筆電❶，你會搞丟。）

　　　　乙回答 I promise I won't.（我保證不會。）

　　　　反問 ＿＿＿＿＿＿＿＿＿＿＿＿＿＿＿＿＿

　　　　甲回答 ＿＿＿＿＿＿＿＿＿＿＿＿＿＿＿＿＿

（再延伸）甲：＿＿＿＿＿＿＿＿＿＿＿＿＿＿＿＿＿

　　　　乙：＿＿＿＿＿＿＿＿＿＿＿＿＿＿＿＿＿

---

❶ 台灣人習慣把中文的「筆記型電腦」說成英文的 "Notebook" 但是英文的這字就是「筆記本」，完全沒有電腦的意思。所謂的「筆記型電腦」就是 laptop。

Special/Urgent Occasions 特殊/緊急狀況

10.　　　播放 It's an emergency. Could you put me through to
　　　　　　the police, please? 暫停

　　甲複誦 It's an emergency. Could you put me through to
　　　　　　the police, please?

　　　　　（這裡有緊急情況，可以請你幫我轉接警察嗎？）

　　乙回答 I'll put you through right now.

　　　　　（我現在就幫你轉接。）

　　　反問　_____

　　甲回答　_____

（再延伸）甲：_____

　　　　乙：_____

---

8. 相關情境

反問：Is there any particular spot you're looking for? 有甚麼特
　　　別想去的地方嗎？

甲回答：Yes, could you tell me the way to Jioufen? 有耶！可否
　　　　告訴我九份怎麼走？

詢問方向

問

Is there a bus stop around? 附近有公車站嗎？

Could you tell me the way to Taipei 101?
可否告訴我 101 大樓怎麼走？

How can I get to this address? 這個地址怎麼走？

答	
It's over there.	就在那裡。
It's on this street.	就在這條街上。
It's on the (right/left) corner.	在右邊／左邊轉角。
It's on the right/left-hand side of the street.	在這條路的右／左邊。
It's the third store from the corner.	轉角數過去第三家店。
It's on the opposite side of the street.	在街對面。
It's across from the street.	在街對面。
It's kitty-corner from the store.	在那家店的斜對面。
It's diagonal to the store.	在那家店的斜對面。
Go straight/right/left. It's straight ahead.	直／右／左走。往前直走就是。
Turn right/left. Take a right/left turn.	左／右轉。

9. 相關情境

反問：When did I break my promise to you?
我哪時違背過對你的承諾？

甲回答：You just did it when you tell Jen the secret.
你才剛告訴珍那個秘密。

承諾的說法

You have to swear. 你一定要發誓。	You have my words of honor. 我以人格保證。
Guarantee it. 要保證。	I cross my heart. 我發誓了。

10. 相關情境

特殊 / 緊急狀況

反問：Is there anything else I can help you?
　　　還有甚麼需要幫忙的嗎？

甲回答：I need ambulance, please.
　　　我需要救護車。

今天還是模擬十題多益問答聽力測驗，然後再就測驗內容延伸對話。

請打開音檔： Mp3 041

1-10 Mark your answer on your answer sheet.

核對答案：

1. C　2. B　3. A　4. A　5. A　6. A　7. C　8. A　9. B　10. B

再播放剛才的測驗內容以延伸對話。 Mp3 042

Procedure and Steps 程序與步驟

1.　　　　**播放** Do you know how to operate the machine?
　　　　暫停

　　　甲複誦 Do you know how to operate the machine?
　　　　　　（你知道如何操作這台機器嗎?）

　　　乙回答 Let me show you.（讓我告訴你。）

　　　反問 _____

　　　甲回答 _____

（再延伸）**甲：** _____

　　　　乙： _____

Procedure and Steps 程序與步驟

2.　　　　播放 What's your schedule like yesterday?

　　　　暫停

　　　　甲複誦 What's your schedule like yesterday?

　　　　　　　（昨天你的行程怎麼樣？）

　　　　乙回答 It's hustle and bustle.（又繁雜又忙碌。）

　　　　反問 _____

　　　　甲回答 _____

（再延伸）甲：_____

　　　　乙：_____

Procedure and Steps 程序與步驟

3.　　　　播放 Before you write a report, first of all, select your topic.

　　　　暫停

　　　　甲複誦 Before you write a report, first of all, select your topic.（寫一份報告之前，首先選擇你的主題。）

　　　　乙問答 OK, what's next?（好啊！然後呢？）

　　　　甲回答 _____

（再延伸）乙：_____

1. 相關情境

乙答問： First, You'll have to put the plug in the socket and then what should you do?

首先，要把插頭插上，接下來你該知道怎麼做了吧？

甲回答： Yah, switch on the machine, but I still don't know what to do next.

唉呀！打開開關嘛！可我還是不知道下一步啊！

乙回答： Then push the button to warm it up.

然後按這個鈕熱機。

甲答問： Oh yes, after that, the instruction will show up on the screen. Then all I have to do is just follow it. Am I right?

喔！對了，然後操作程序就會顯示在螢幕上，然後我只要照著指示做就好了，對嗎？

程序與步驟的列舉

1. Ordinal number 序數法：

   First, second, third, fourth, fifth, sixth... ninth, tenth, eleventh... twenty-first... 等等。

2. Steps + cardinal number 步驟＋基數法：

   Step one, step two, step three... 等等。

3. Adverbial connectives 連接副詞及片語：

   To begin with, next, then, after that, at last, meanwhile, eventually, finally... 等等。

2. 相關情境

乙答問：How about yours? 你的行程呢？

甲回答：Almost the same. I had a long list to get through.
和你差不多。我有一長串的工作清單要完成。

乙回答：Really? What did you have to do?
真的嗎？你必須要做些什麼？

甲答：I had to visit all the committee members coming to my oral defense. Then I went over my thesis again and again, and there were still some errors found. Finally, I was busied overnight with all these made-up works until I saw you.
我必須去拜訪我的論文口試委員會所有成員。然後一遍又一遍檢查我的論文，仍發現了一些錯誤。最後，我忙了這些修潤的工作一整夜，直到看見了你。

3. 相關情境

甲回答：Then find all the available data supporting your topic.
然後找到所有可用的資料去支持你的主題。

乙答：That's exactly my problem. I chose the topic, but the supporting materials are hard to find.
這是正是我的問題。我選了這個主題，但可支援的資料很難找到。

Procedure and Steps 程序與步驟

4.　　　播放 If you find something wrong, just cross it out.

暫停

甲複誦 If you find something wrong, just cross it out.

（如果你發現有什麼錯誤，就把它劃掉。）

乙回答 What if I think it's right?

（如果我認為它是正確的呢？）

甲回答 ＿＿＿＿＿＿＿＿＿＿＿＿＿＿＿＿

（再延伸）乙：＿＿＿＿＿＿＿＿＿＿＿＿＿＿＿＿

Procedure and Steps 程序與步驟

5.　　　播放 The sign indicates the room for the meeting.

暫停

甲複誦 The sign indicates the room for the meeting.

（那標誌顯示這是會議室。）

乙回答 Oh, thanks.（噢，謝謝。）

反問 ＿＿＿＿＿＿＿＿＿＿＿＿＿＿＿＿

甲回答 ＿＿＿＿＿＿＿＿＿＿＿＿＿＿＿＿

Music 音樂

6.　　　播放 Can you turn down the TV?　暫停

甲複誦 Can you turn down the TV?

（你可以把電視關小聲一點嗎？）

乙回答 But I can hardly hear it!（但是我快聽不到了！）

反問 ＿＿＿＿＿＿＿＿＿＿＿＿＿＿＿＿

　　　　甲回答 _____

（再延伸）乙：_____

School Life 學校生活

7.　　　　播放 How come you always come to class so early?
　　　　暫停

　　甲複誦 How come you always come to class so early?
　　　　（怎麼你總是這麼早來上課？）

　　乙回答 I never stay up late.（我從不熬夜。）
　　　反問 _____
　　甲回答 _____

（再延伸）甲：_____
　　　　乙：_____

【Day 4】Thursday

---

4. 相關情境

甲回答：Then you can just keep on doing. 然後你可以繼續做。

乙答：I mean I'm not sure if it's right.
　　　我的意思是我不確定它是否正確。

---

5. 相關情境

反問：Then where is the room for presentation?
　　　那麼演說室在哪裡？

甲答：I will show you next. 接下來我會告訴你。

---

6. 相關情境

乙反問：It's so funny. I thought you liked this music, too.
這曲子蠻好玩的。我以為你也喜歡這種音樂。

甲答：I do like it, but it's not the right time to listen to. The soothing music is better now. 我喜歡它，但現在不是聽的時候。現在比較適合撫慰的音樂。

乙答：All right! I now put on my headphone.
好吧！我現在戴上我的耳機。

談音樂

I listen to rock music before I get ready for work. It can sober me up! 我準備上班之前都聽搖滾音樂。它能讓我清醒！

I'd rather drink strong coffee to wake up.
我寧願喝濃咖啡來提神。

I prefer classical music to make the sense clearer.
我更喜歡古典音樂，使理智更加清醒。

7. 相關情境
乙反問：How come you always late? 那你怎麼總是遲到？
甲答：I always stay up late. 我總是熬夜。
甲問：How can you sleep so well when everybody is playing music in the dormitory? 當每個人都在宿舍玩音樂時，怎麼你能睡得這麼好？
乙答：I wear my earplugs. 我戴了耳塞。

上課遲到的對話

Why are you late this morning? 你今天早上為什麼遲到？	Sorry, I missed my train. 對不起，我沒趕上火車。
Where have you been the last hour? 上個小時你在那裡？	I was in the restroom. 我是在洗手間裡。
We've started for twenty minutes. 我們已經開始二十分鐘了。	I'm really sorry. There was a traffic jam. 我真的很抱歉。有交通堵塞。

School Life 學校生活

8.　　　　　播放 Have you ever taken lessons before?　暫停

　　甲複誦 Have you ever taken lessons before?

　　　　　（你以前曾經上過課嗎？）

　　乙回答 Yes, long time ago.（是啊，很久以前。）

　　反問 ＿＿＿＿＿＿＿＿＿＿＿＿＿＿＿＿＿＿＿＿

　　甲回答 ＿＿＿＿＿＿＿＿＿＿＿＿＿＿＿＿＿＿＿＿

　　乙：＿＿＿＿＿＿＿＿＿＿＿＿＿＿＿＿＿＿＿＿

Music 音樂

9.　　　　播放 What do you think of the music?　暫停

　　　甲複誦 What do you think of the music?

　　　　　（你覺得這音樂怎麼樣？）

　　　乙回答 It's soothing.（很撫慰人心。）

　　　反問 _____

　　　甲回答 _____

（再延伸）甲： _____

　　　乙： _____

Music 音樂

10.　　　　播放 Do you recognize this love song?　暫停

　　　甲複誦 Do you recognize this love song?

　　　　　（你聽過得這首情歌嗎？）

　　　乙回答 I've never heard it before.（沒聽過。）

　　　反問 _____

　　　甲回答 _____

（再延伸）甲： _____

　　　乙： _____

8. 相關情境

反問：What kind of music does this class teach?

這個班教的是什麼樣的音樂？

甲答：Mostly pop music. What kind of instrument do you play?

主要是流行音樂。你玩什麼樂器？

乙：I play the piano, but I also play pop songs.

我彈鋼琴，但是我也玩流行歌曲。

9. 相關情境

反問：And you? Does it touch you?

你呢？它感動你了嗎？

甲答：It might help me get to sleep at night.

它可能有助於我晚上睡個好覺。

甲：So you prefer soft songs?

所以你比較喜歡柔和的歌曲嗎？

乙：Not exactly, I also like classical music, and it isn't always soft. 不盡然，我也喜歡古典音樂，但它並不都是柔和的。

10. 相關情境

反問：Does it remind you anything? 它讓你回想起任何事情嗎？

甲答：Yes, it makes me think of my first girlfriend.
是的，它使我想起了我的第一任女朋友。

甲：Are you sure that you really don't have any idea of the song?
你確定你真的對這首歌沒有任何概念？

乙：My heart is broken again. You really don't remember that this is the first song I invited you to dance?
我的心又碎了。你真的不記得這是我邀請你跳舞的第一首歌嗎？

音樂的形容詞彙

a real pleasure to listen to（真正歡愉的聆聽）

tender voice（細膩的聲音）

heavenly tune（天籟般的曲調）

soul-stirring piece of music（撼動靈魂的絕響）

hypnotic vocal tone（令人神往的音色）

amazing quality（絕妙的音質）

taking things to a whole other level（帶領心神到另一個境界）

breathtakingly beautiful（令人驚歎的美妙）

我們最後再模擬十題多益問答聽力測驗，然後再就測驗內容延伸對話。

請打開音檔：🎧 Mp3 043

1-10 Mark your answer on your answer sheet.

核對答案：

1. C　2. C　3. B　4. B　5. A　6. B　7. A　8. B　9. C　10. A

再播放剛才的測驗內容以延伸對話。🎧 Mp3 044

Team Activity 團隊活動

1.　　　　　播放 Do you have any idea where our team is?　暫停

　　　甲複誦 Do you have any idea where our team is?

　　　　　　（你知道我們的團隊在哪裡嗎？）

　　　乙回答 The one in blue.

　　　　　　（穿藍色球衣的就是。）

　　　　反問 ＿＿＿＿＿＿＿＿＿＿＿＿＿＿＿＿＿＿＿

　　　甲回答 ＿＿＿＿＿＿＿＿＿＿＿＿＿＿＿＿＿＿＿

（再延伸）甲：＿＿＿＿＿＿＿＿＿＿＿＿＿＿＿＿＿＿＿

　　　　乙：＿＿＿＿＿＿＿＿＿＿＿＿＿＿＿＿＿＿＿

Team Activity 團隊活動

2.　　　　　播放 Which one is his?　暫停

　　　甲複誦 Which one is his?（哪一個是他的？）

　　　乙回答 Let me see them.（讓我看看。）

　　　　反問 ＿＿＿＿＿＿＿＿＿＿＿＿＿＿＿＿＿＿＿

　　　甲回答 ＿＿＿＿＿＿＿＿＿＿＿＿＿＿＿＿＿＿＿

　（再延伸）甲：＿＿＿＿＿＿＿＿＿＿＿＿＿＿＿＿＿＿＿

　　　　　乙：＿＿＿＿＿＿＿＿＿＿＿＿＿＿＿＿＿＿＿

Team Activity 團隊活動

3.　　　　　播放 How well do you think we will do?　暫停

　　　甲複誦 How well do you think we will do?

　　　　　　　（你覺得他們可以表現多好？）

　　　乙回答 We will be hard to beat.（我們是很難打敗的。）

　　　　反問 ＿＿＿＿＿＿＿＿＿＿＿＿＿＿＿＿＿＿＿

　　　甲回答 ＿＿＿＿＿＿＿＿＿＿＿＿＿＿＿＿＿＿＿

　（再延伸）甲：＿＿＿＿＿＿＿＿＿＿＿＿＿＿＿＿＿＿＿

　　　　　乙：＿＿＿＿＿＿＿＿＿＿＿＿＿＿＿＿＿＿＿

【Day 5】
Friday

1. 相關情境

反問：Who is winning? 誰領先？

甲答：Our team. 我們的隊。

甲：How well do you think they will do? 你覺得他們可以表現多好？

乙：They might even get better scores this year. 他們今年甚至可能拿到更好的分數。

看比賽的說法

The girls must be on the same team.
那些女孩們一定是同一隊的。（注意介系詞）

The players are not in the game on the court.
球員們沒上球場參賽。（注意介系詞）

They are waiting on the bench❷.
他們在板凳上等。（注意介系詞）

The boy is watching his teammates.
那個男孩正在看他的隊友們。

Which teams are playing? 哪兩個隊在比賽？

What is the score? 比數多少？

Who won the game? 誰贏了這場比賽？

---

❷ 等待參賽的隊員通常坐在長凳上，若坐久了遲遲不見上場，就會讓人譏諷是「坐冷板凳」，也就是「暖凳者」（bench warmer）的來源。

2. 相關情境

反問：These caps all look similar. I can't tell which one belongs to my boy.
這些帽子都是一個樣子。我認不出哪一個是我兒子的。

甲答：See if he put the name under the visor. 看看他是否在帽簷下寫了名字。

甲：Yes, here it is. Is this Jeremy's?
是的，它在這兒。這是傑瑞米的嗎？

乙：Let me see. It's the right name, but not the same handwriting. There must be two or more Jeremies.
讓我看看。名字對了，但筆跡不同。一定還有兩個或更多的傑瑞米。

3. 相關情境

反問：Do you know what our records for wins❸ or losses are?
你知道我們的勝負記錄嗎？

甲答：I have no idea. 不知道。

乙：We haven't lost a match this year. 今年我們還沒有敗績。

甲：So today the game on the court must be interesting.
所以今天球場上的比賽一定會很有趣的。

---

❸ 中文的「我贏你」，英文是 "I beat you"（我打敗你）而沒有 "I win you" 的說法。Win, Lose 只能表達贏得與輸掉的事物，如輸掉或贏得比賽 / 戰鬥 "win or lose the game/ battle"。

Team Activity 團隊活動

4. 　　播放 Who is this present for?　暫停

　　甲複誦 Who is this present for?（這禮物是給誰的？）

　　乙回答 It could be for Tom.（可能是給湯姆的。）

　　反問 _____

　　甲回答 _____

（再延伸）甲： _____

　　乙： _____

Team Activity 團隊活動

5. 　　播放 A lot of players are on the field!　暫停

　　甲複誦 A lot of players are on the field!

　　　　　（球場上有很多球員！）

　　乙回答 Some of them will play.（有些人會參賽。）

　　反問 _____

　　甲回答 _____

（再延伸）甲： _____

　　乙： _____

Meetings會議

6. 　　播放 As a chairman, I'd like to call this meeting to order.　暫停

　　甲複誦 As a chairman, I'd like to call this meeting to order.（作為主席，我想宣布這次會議開始。）

　　乙回答 But Bill and Sue are not here yet.

　　　　　（但比爾和蘇尚未到場。）

反問	_____
甲回答	_____
（再延伸）乙：	_____
丙：	_____

---

4. 相關情境

反問：What's wrong with the present? 禮物有什麼不對嗎？

甲答：I can't figure out whose birthday is today.
我想不出今天是誰生日。

乙：Oh! You were on the vacation, so you don't know we are celebrating the championship Tom won for us.
哦！你在假期中，所以你不知道我們正在慶祝湯姆為我們贏得了冠軍。

甲：Is there anything else I missed? 我還錯過了什麼嗎？

---

5. 相關情境

反問：Have you been watching football game?

甲答：Yes, my favorite team is Buffalo Bills
是的，我最喜歡的球隊是水牛城比爾隊。

乙：Aren't they the champion of the Super Bowl last year?
他們不是去年超級盃冠軍嗎？

甲：Yes, they are the one. 是的，就是他們。

【Day 5】
Friday

6. 相關情境

反問：Maybe we can wait for a little while.
也許我們可以再等一小會兒。

甲答：Ok! Since this is a very important meeting for us, we need every officer to make it. 好吧！因為這是非常重要的會議，對我們來說，我們需要每個幹部都能出席。

乙：Here they are! Hurry up! We have been expecting you for a while. 他們到了！快點！我們已經等你們一段時間了。

丙：Sorry, the traffic is really horrible!
對不起，交通狀況真的遭透了！

籌備會議的說法

I'm just calling to organize a budget conference.
我就是召集大家來籌備一次預算會議。

We will discuss the new logo at our next project meeting.
我們將在下一次專案會議討論新的標誌。

I was ringing to fix up the coming board meeting.
我在召集著籌備即將到來的董事會會議。

We are going to have a brainstorming meeting. 我們即將召開一次腦力激盪會議。

I need you to decide on the date of AGM (annual general meeting). 我需要你們來決定年度股東大會（年會）的日期。

Meetings會議

7.　　　　播放 Who is the treasurer of the corporation?　暫停

　　　甲複誦 Who is the treasurer of the corporation?

　　　　　　（該公司的財務主管是誰？）

　　　乙回答 I don't know.（我不知道。）

　　　　反問 _____

　　　甲回答 _____

（再延伸）甲：_____

　　　　乙：_____

Meetings會議

8.　　　　播放 You must be thrilled on a roll.　暫停

　　　甲複誦 You must be thrilled on a roll.

　　　　　　（接二連三地獲得成功，一定讓你非常興奮。）

　　　乙回答 I just hit my winning streak.

　　　　　　（我正好遇上了好事連連。）

　　　　反問 _____

　　　甲回答 _____

（再延伸）甲：_____

　　　　乙：_____

Meetings會議

9.　　　　播放　Secretarial job is my least favorite work of all!

　　　　暫停

　　　　甲複誦　Secretarial job is my least favorite work of all!

　　　　　　　（秘書是所有的工作中，我最不喜歡的！）

　　　　乙反問　What else can you do?

　　　　　　　（你能做些什麼別的呢？）

　　　　甲回答　_____

　　（再延伸）甲：_____

　　　　　乙：_____

Meetings會議

10.　　　　播放　What if no people join us?　暫停

　　　　甲複誦　What if no people join us?

　　　　　　　（如果沒有人加入我們怎麼辦？）

　　　　乙回答　I doubt that will happen.（我想這該不會發生。）

　　　　反問　_____

　　　　甲回答　_____

　　（再延伸）甲：_____

　　　　　乙：_____

7. 相關情境

反問：I thought you were the last one. Aren't you? 你是前一任財務長，不是嗎？

甲答：Yes I was, but I have kept my hands off their business since I left.
是的，但自從我離開後，我已經完全不管他們的公司了。

乙：What did you do when you are their treasurer?
當你是他們的財務主管時，你都做些什麼？

甲：Just cut almost all the budgets for more shareholders' income. 就是幾乎削減所有的預算來增加股東更多的收入。

8. 相關情境

反問：How are your chances lately? 最近機遇如何？

甲答：Not as smooth as yours. 不如你一樣的平順。

乙：Every dog has his/its day. I am just lucky to get mine.
每條狗都有好運的一天。我只是幸運而已。

甲：Yes, every cloud has a silver lining. My clouds are getting away.
是的，每一朵雲都鑲了銀邊（意為撥雲見日）。我的烏雲快離開了。

【Day 5】
Friday

9. 相關情境

甲答：I used to be a good salesman finding new customers and follow up on existing customers. 我曾經是一個好的推銷員，尋找新客戶，並和舊客戶維持良好關係。

乙：Do you have the opportunity to generate our sales leads? 你有機會去開發我們的商機嗎？

甲：Certainly, I would locate potential customers and set up meetings with them to introduce our new products. 當然，我會找到潛在客戶並邀約他們會面，介紹我們的新產品。

10. 相關情境

反問：What do you think all the funds came for? 你認為所有的贊助金是來幹什麼的？

甲答：It's just too quiet. We haven't seen anyone register our membership yet. 只是太安靜了。還沒有看到任何人來註冊我們的會員。

乙：Just cross the bridge when you come to it. 船到橋頭自然直。

甲：I hope so. 但願如此。

附錄

錄音稿 Week 1 Day 1 (Monday)

MP3 01

Picture Description

Listen and choose the statement that best describes what you see in the picture.

1. (A) There are two signs near the tree.
   (B) The sign is behind the tree.
   (C) This tree has a bell on it.
   (D) No trees can be seen in the court.

2. (A) The man is walking beside the car.
   (B) There are hundreds of cars on the street.
   (C) The man is wearing a shirt.
   (D) Some tattoos can be seen on the man's back.

3. (A) The roof is planted with flowers.
   (B) Three poles are at the bottom of the roof.
   (C) The people are far away from the roof.
   (D) The day is sunny.

4. (A) There are a trio of dancers on the stage.
   (B) All of them are in black.
   (C) The audience is paying attention to the performance.
   (D) They are all playing rings in front of the audience.

5. (A) The woods are near the river.
   (B) The bridge is in the middle of water.
   (C) There is no passengers in the center of the bridge.
   (D) There is a weeping willow on top of the bridge.

6. (A) This is a toy crane.
   (B) This is a real crane.
   (C) This is a statue of a crane.
   (D) This is a crane in the air.

7. (A) Three rhinos are playing under the shade.
   (B) There are no trees around the rhinos.
   (C) They are walking around the yard.
   (D) Two of the rhinos are sleeping.

8. (A) The bridge is on the top of mountains.
   (B) The bridge stretches across the stream.
   (C) The stream is close by the bridge.
   (D) The bridge is at the end of the valley.

9. (A) Some passengers are ready to jump.
   (B) The suspension bridge has a red tower.
   (C) One of the passengers is under the suspension bridge.
   (D) No passenger is passing the suspension bridge.
10. (A) The swans are flying.
   (B) The swans are following the ducks.
   (C) They are fighting on the lake.
   (D) They are sitting in a circle.

MP3 02
Repeat the following accented words. (Capitals stand for the stress)

HOTdog	hot DOG	GREENbelt	green BELT
BAREback	bare BACK	BLUEgrass	blue GRASS
BLACKberry	black BERRY	HIGH top	high TOP
BOLDface	bold FACE	DARKroom	dark ROOM
ODDball	odd BALL	REDcoat*	red COAT
GREENhouse	green HOUSE		

··

錄音稿 **Week 1 Day2 (Tuesday)**

MP3 03

For questions number 1 and 2, please look at picture A.

Question number 1: What does the picture show?
   A. It's hot and rainy today.
   B. They're looking at a view.
   C. They're washing a suit.
   D. There are a lot of swimmers in the water.

Question number 2: Which description matches the picture?
   A. They all have short hair.
   B. They are wearing hats.
   C. The girl has long hair.
   D. The boy is wearing short pants.

For question number 3, please look at picture B.

Question number 3: A bakery is preparing Dorayaki. Which of the following information is true?

A. The cup is in front of the table.

B. The red beans are filled inside the Dorayaki.

C. A wallet with flowers is on the front.

D. There are flowers inside the cup.

For question number 4, please look at picture C.

Question number 4: Which description matches the picture?

    A. The statue is next to the girl.

    B. The girl is in front of the statue.

    C. The TV is across from the statue.

    D. The TV is next to the girl.

For questions number 5 to 7, please look at picture D.

Question number 5: Look at Joanna. What's she holding?

    A. She's holding a scoop.

    B. She's holding a raincoat.

    C. She's holding a hood.

    D. She's holding a pack.

Question number 6: Look at Joanna again. What is she doing?

    A. She's cutting the plant.

    B. She's sweeping the floor.

    C. She's piling up some dirt.

    D. She's digging the soil.

Question number 7: Look at the two persons behind Joanna. What are they wearing?

    A. They are wearing shorts.

    B. They are wearing skirts.

    C. They are wearing gloves.

    D. They are wearing raincoats.

For questions number 8 and 9, please look at picture E.

Question number 8: A boy is in a classroom. What are in front of him?

    A. Two buckets of water.

    B. Two bucks on a counter.

    C. Tools on the table.

    D. Two washing machines.

Question number 9: What does the classroom look like?
  A. There're no signs in the front of the classroom.
  B. There's a teacher in the front of the classroom.
  C. On the front, you can see a black poster with signs.
  D. There're no posters on the wall.

For question number 10, please look at picture F.
  Question number 10: How are the wooden zebras located?
  A. They're behind the beverage vending machines.
  B. They're in front of the scooters.
  C. One of them is in front of the billboard.
  D. One of them is next to the billboard.

For questions number 11 and 12, please look at picture G.
Question number 11: What do the cages show?
  A. There're two dogs in the cages.
  B. The dog is in a vest.
  C. The cages are all made of wood.
  D. The cages are all made of steel.
Question number 12: Look at the cages again. Where is the dog looking?
  A. He is looking at his left.
  B. He is looking at his right.
  C. He is looking forward.
  D. He is looking behind.

For question number 13, please look at picture H.
Question number 13: What are they probably doing?
  A. Talking with the lady behind them.
  B. Waiting to check in far from the counter.
  C. Waiting to check in near the counter.
  D. Shopping in the convenience store.

For question number 14, please look at picture I.
Question number 14: What's the traffic situation on the highway?
  A. A car was hit by a truck, so traffic is moving very slowly.
  B. The highway is closed for road maintenance.

C. Traffic is moving quite smoothly at this time of the day.

D. There's been an accident. A car has just hit the rail.

For question number 15, please look at picture J.

Question number 15: Which instructions match the pictures?

A. The train has arrived. All passengers please alight.

B. The doors are about to close. Please keep clear of the doors.

C. The train is arriving. Please get ready to board.

D. Here we are at the terminal station. Thank you for your patronage.

．．

錄音稿 Week 1 Day 3 (Wednesday)

MP3 04

Picture Description

Look and choose the statement that best describes what you see in the picture.

1. A. They are jogging on the tracks.

   B. They are walking on the tracks.

   C. The woman is walking in the field.

   D. The weather is cloudy.

2. A. The bird on the top is walking.

   B. The bird on the floor is walking.

   C. The bird on the top is dancing.

   D. Bird on the floor is singing.

3. A. The man is sitting in the horse-drawn carriage.

   B. The horse is running away.

   C. The man is sitting in the front of the carriage.

   D. They are having a picnic in a park.

4. A. The woman is sleeping in the room.

   B. The woman is weaving by the loom.

   C. The woman is sweeping the broom.

   D. The woman is sitting on the broom.

5. A. The men are sitting at the table.

   B. The ash tray is on the floor.

   C. The table is behind them.

   D. The man is talking to the woman.

6. A. There is a price sign beside the stand.

   B. The stand is full of vegetables.

C. The stand is full of fruits.

D. The price is two thousand and two hundred.

7. A. The sky is clear.

   B. There is only one boat on the sea.

   C. The boats are full of fish.

   D. The weather is cloudy.

8. A. The woman is waiting by the stand.

   B. The woman is buying something.

   C. The stand is full of books.

   D. The woman is cleaning the table.

9. A. The tree stands in the path.

   B. The path is crowded with people.

   C. The path is paved across the lawn.

   D. The path is surrounded by water.

10. A. The horse is probably waiting for his passenger.

    B. The horse is walking on the street.

    C. The horse is ridden by a man.

    D. The horse is eating by the road.

....

錄音稿 Week 1 Day 4 (Thursday)

* Stress underlined syllables.

MP3 05

They're drying cloths.

They're drying cloths.

They're hiking trails.

They're hiking trails.

They're planning meetings.

They're planning meetings.

They're racing bikes.

They're racing bikes.

They're sailing ships.

They're sailing ships.

They're <u>advertising</u> companies.
They're advertising <u>companies</u>.

They're <u>mailing</u> envelopes.
They're mailing <u>envelopes</u>.

They're <u>cutting</u> boards.
They're cutting <u>boards</u>.

MP3 06

Picture Description

Listen and choose the statement that best describes what you see in the picture.

1. **Look at picture No. 1.**
   (A) The boy is smiling.
   (B) The boy is wearing a cap.
   (C) The girl is crying.
   (D) <u>The girl is wearing a hat.</u>

2. **Look at picture No. 2.**
   (A) People are in a flea market.
   (B) <u>People are in an arcade.</u>
   (C) People are in a department store.
   (D) There is no crowd in this picture.

3. **Look at picture No. 3.**
   (A) A girl is washing a pan.
   (B) <u>A girl is cooking with pan.</u>
   (C) A girl is turning the pan.
   (D) A girl is searching for the pan.

4. **Look at picture No. 4.**
   (A) The path is crowded.
   (B) There are two statues in the caves.
   (C) <u>The caves are behind the waterfall.</u>
   (D) The girls are chatting in front of a fountain.

5. **Look at picture No. 5.**
   (A) The trees are real plants.
   (B) <u>The trees are bound with barrier tapes.</u>

(C) The trees are surrounded with people.

(D) The trees are blocked by police.

6. **Look at picture No. 6.**

(A) The swings are behind the tree.

(B) The path is behind the tree.

(C) Two boys are playing on the swings.

(D) The ladders are close to the tree.

7. **Look at picture No. 7.**

(A) The stilt walker is kicking the crowds.

(B) The stilt walker is holding an umbrella.

(C) The woman is helping him up.

(D) All of the crowds are walking stilts.

8. **Look at picture No. 8.**

(A) The statue is wearing a jacket.

(B) The statue is holding a bat.

(C) They are walking on the street.

(D) They are lifting a statue on their shoulders.

9. **Look at picture No. 9.**

(A) The woman is ready to jump.

(B) The woman is waving her hand.

(C) The woman is chatting with the others.

(D) The woman is lying on the float.

10. **Look at picture No.10.**

(A) Some people are playing behind basketball stands.

(B) The court is full of basketballs.

(C) A man is standing by the basketball stands.

(D) They are standing at the main gate.

••

錄音稿 **Week 1 Day 5**

(pause 3 seconds after each word or phrase)

MP3 07

1. above, against, among, at, at the back of, at the end of, atop, before, behind, below, beneath, between, by, close to, in, inside, in front of, near, next to, on, on top of, over, under

••

MP3 08

2.

A.

cleaning, crossing, cutting, drawing, drinking, eating, holding, jogging, listening, loading, locking, making, packing, playing, pouring, pulling, pushing, selling, setting, sitting, speaking, stretching, sweeping, talking, typing, walking, watching, watering, working, wrapping, writing

B.

being + cleaned, cleared, displayed, dug up, handed, locked, painted, planted, poled, pilled, served, set up, towed, walked, washed, watered, wrapped

MP3 09

3.

A.

afraid, asleep, beautiful, bent, bright, clean, dark, dirty, empty, flat, full, happy, heavy, high, light, long, open, rainy, round, tall, sad, straight, wet

B.

arranged, blocked, broken, chained, cleared, closed, crowded, crushed, deserted, displayed, equipped, loaded, occupied, parked, piled, posted, scattered, seated, stacked, stranded, tried

MP3 10

4.

A.

afford / offer, awful / oval, ball / bawl, bike / hike, cheer / chair, clean / lean, coach / couch, hitting / fitting, just / adjust, lake / rake, lamp / ramp, law / raw, lean / learn, light / right, lock / rock, low / row, owl / foul, mail / rail, meal / wheal, on the / under, peach / speech, peel / pill, pine / fine, player / prayer, playing / plane, pool / pull, poor / four, possible / impossible, rag / bag, selling / sailing, sheer / share, shopping / chopping, talk / take, there / they're, try / tie, wait / weigh, walk / work, west / rest, wheel / will

B.

aboard / abroad / board, inboard / onboard, agree / disagree, appear / disappear, aware / unaware, close / enclose, extract / exhale, just / adjust, relay / delay, reread / relayed, rest / arrest, similar / dissimilar, terrible /

terrific, tie / untie, tire / retire, type / retype, underworked / underused, undrinkable / unthinkable

···

(The CAPITALS stand for the stresses)

MP3 11

Picture Description

Look and choose the statement that best describes what you see in the picture.

1. What does the picture show?
   A. The woman is on the BAREback.
   B. The horse is running with bare feet.
   C. The woman is running the horse.
   D. The woman is riding with bare BACK.

2. Which description matches the picture?
   A. Everyone on the street is walking with bare BACK.
   B. The man is riding a motorcycle.
   C. The bare BACK man is walking.
   D. All of the motorcycles have BARE backs.

3. Which of the following answers best describe the picture?
   A. The passage is written in French.
   B. The passage is written in bold FACE.
   C. "Like this, and this" are written in BOLDface.
   D. The passage is written by a man with bold FACE.

4. Which of the following answers best describes the picture?
   A. It's a bold FACE of a woman.
   B. It's a bold FACE of a man.
   C. The bold FACE has long hair.
   D. The bold FACE wears a long beard.

5. Which of the following answers best describe the picture?
   A. The plants are all in the GREENhouse.
   B. There is no one in the GREENhouse.
   C. The GREENhouse is full of plants.
   D. There are a lot of flowers in the greenHOUSE.

6. Which of the following answers best describe the picture?
   A. The plants are all in the GREENhouse.
   B. There is a man in the greenHOUSE.

C. The GREENhouse is in a city.

D. There are a lot of flowers around the greenHOUSE.

7. Which of the following answers best describe the picture?

    A. The cowboys are chasing sheep and cattle.

    B. The cowboys are herding cattle and sheep on the GREENbelt.

    C. It's raining on the GREENbelt.

    D. There is nothing on the green BELT.

8. Which of the following answers best describe the picture?

    A. The karate fighter is in a suit.

    B. The fighter has a karate green BELT.

    C. The karate fighter wears a glove.

    D. The karate fighter is on a GREENbelt.

9. Which of the following answers best describe the picture?

    A. The basketball player is in swimsuit.

    B. The basketball player is in boots.

    C. There are a pair of HIGH top sneakers by the player.

    D. The basketball player is on the high TOP.

10. Which of the following answers best describe the picture?

    A. The woman is cheering on the high TOP.

    B. The woman is flying in the sky.

    C. There is nothing on the high TOP.

    D. The woman is in HIGH top.

錄音稿 Week 2　Day 1 (Monday)

MP3 12

Taiwan's democracy / has been treading down a rocky road, / but now it has finally won the chance / to enter a smoother path. / During that difficult time, / political trust was low, / political maneuvering was high, / and economic security was gone. / Support for Taiwan from abroad / had suffered an all-time low. / Fortunately, / the growing pains of Taiwan's democracy / did not last long / compared to those of other young democracies. / Through these growing pains, / Taiwan's democracy matured as one can see / by the clear choice the people / made at this critical moment. / The people have chosen clean politics, / an open economy, / ethnic harmony, / and peaceful cross-strait relations / to open their arms to the future.

Above all, / the people have rediscovered / Taiwan's traditional core values / of benevolence, / righteousness, diligence, / honesty, generosity and industriousness. / This remarkable experience has let Taiwan / become "a beacon of democracy to Asia and the world. / " We, / the people of Taiwan, / should be proud of ourselves. / The Republic of China / is now a democracy / respected by the international community.

Yet we are still not content. / We must better Taiwan's democracy, / enrich its substance, and make it more perfect. / To accomplish this, / we can rely on the Constitution to protect human rights, / uphold law and order, / make justice independent and impartial, / and breathe new life into civil society. / Taiwan's democracy should not be marred by illegal eavesdropping, / arbitrary justice, / and political interference / in the media or electoral institutions. / All of us share this vision / for the next phase / of political reform.

∙∙∙

MP3 13

democracy [di`mkrəsi]          particular [pə`tikjələ]
individual [ˌɪndə`vidʒʊəl]       historic [his`tɔrik]
milestone [`mailˌston]          treading down [`trɛdɪŋ `daʊn]

∙∙∙

錄音稿 **Week 2 Day 2 (Tuesday)**

MP3 14

Directions: In this part of the test, you will read aloud the text on the screen. You will have 45 seconds to prepare. Then you will have 45 seconds to read the text aloud.

Question 1 of 11

The park is located in a quiet mountain valley where a clear stream wanders through. Stroll along the trail and you will see layers of unsophisticated paddy fields while birds sing in harmony with the flowing waters. Between late summer and early autumn, blooming wild ginger lilies turn this place into an aromatic white paradise on earth.

Directions: In this part of the test, you will read aloud the text on the screen. You will have 45 seconds to prepare. Then you will have 45 seconds to read the text aloud.

Question 2 of 11

The Teenagers' Institute at National University in Taiwan released a survey yesterday on teenagers' favorite form of entertainment. In this survey, 2,100 teenagers in Taipei City were interviewed. 39% of the respondents say that they spend most of their free time playing computer games. 30% of the teenagers taking the survey say they like to go to movies or concerts.

MP3 15

Directions: In this part of the test, you will read aloud the text on the screen. You will have 45 seconds to prepare. Then you will have 45 seconds to read the text aloud.

Question 1 of 11

From north to south, the unique rock formations of the Northeast Coast come to an end within the waves and rock forests of Beiguan. Here, cliffs standing bravely through battering waves present a uniform and graceful cuesta landform, while tofu rocks distributed over cuestas in chessboard form glow under the sun.

Directions: In this part of the test, you will read aloud the text on the screen. You will have 45 seconds to prepare. Then you will have 45 seconds to read the text aloud.

Question 2 of 11

The size of the average Japanese family has become smaller. According to a report, there were usually four people in most families thirty years ago; that is to say, parents and two children. In 2012, however, 40% of married couples usually had one child. The other 60% of the couples said they didn't want to have children. Obviously, families in Japan nowadays have fewer children than in the past.

MP3 16

Directions: In this part of the test, you will read aloud the text on the screen. You will have 45 seconds to prepare. Then you will have 45 seconds to read the text aloud.

Question 1 of 11

Be careful. We have a cold front coming. Tomorrow is a day to stay home if you can. There will be snow falling all day, heavy at times, and strong winds. The roads will be in a bad condition, so don't drive if you don't have to. Since it will be very cold all day and through the night, if you must go outside, don't forget the hats, scarves, and gloves. The high temperature tomorrow will be only minus one degree Celsius and the low will be minus three.

Directions: In this part of the test, you will read aloud the text on the screen. You will have 45 seconds to prepare. Then you will have 45 seconds to read the text aloud.

Question 2 of 11

Thank you for calling Bank of Taiwan. All of our representatives are busy at the moment. Please stay on the line and your call will be answered shortly. For reporting a lost credit (debit) card please press 1. For information on credit cards, please press 2. For loan applications, please press 3. For personal investment plans, please press 4. To hear these selections again, please press 5.

∙∙∙

錄音檔 Week 2 Day 3 (Wednesday)

MP3 17

Picture Description

Repeat the statements that describe the picture.

1. (A) There are two signs behind the tree.
   (B) The sign is behind the tree.
   (C) This tree has a lamp on it.
   (D) Parasols can be seen in the court.
2. (A) The man is walking far behind the car.
   (B) There are hundreds of motorcycles on the street.
   (C) The man is shirtless / bare-chested.
   (D) Some tattoos can be seen on the man's back.
3. (A) The roof is planted with flowers.
   (B) Three poles are on top of the roof.
   (C) The crowds are near under the eaves.
   (D) The day is cloudy.
4. (A) There are four dancers on the stage.
   (B) The dancers are holding red flags.
   (C) The audience is paying attention to the show.

(D) One performer is playing a ring in front of the audience.

5. (A) The woods are far behind the river bank.

(B) The bridge is in the middle of water.

(C) There are three passengers in the center of the bridge.

(D) There is a weeping willow at the end of the bridge.

6. (A) The cranes are behind the fence.

(B) There are a flock of cranes.

(C) The yard is swampy.

(D) A crane stands still.

7. (A) Three rhinos are under the shade.

(B) The trees are around the rhinos.

(C) They are resting in the yard.

(D) Two of the rhinos are sleeping.

8. (A) The bridge connects mountains.

(B) The bridge stretches across the stream.

(C) The stream is far below the bridge.

(D) The bridge is in the middle of the valley.

9. (A) Some passengers are passing the bridge.

(B) The suspension bridge has a red tower.

(C) The bridge is hung by two cables.

(D) There are rails by the sides of the cable-stayed bridge.

10. (A) The swans are swimming.

(B) The swans are following the ducks.

(C) They are crossing the river.

(D) There is an arch bridge across the river.

What are there in beach A and beach B? Try to compare them.

11. Beach A

(1) Hot, beautiful, refreshing air.

(2) Heavenly sandy beach.

(3) The breeze is touching every grain of sand.

(4) The sky is idyllic, blue and clear.

(5) The beautiful, big blue ocean's waves are crashing to the cliffs.

12. Beach B

(1) The warm, golden sands, your toes.

(2) The gentle breeze.

(3) You sit alone.

(4) You find gorgeous, shiny shells.

(5) The shells have been washed into the shore by the rippling of the water.

··

MP3 18
Complete Description
1.

There is a court in front of a restaurant. Two signs can be seen behind the tree which has a lamp on it. Tables with parasols are empty now.

2.

A man is shirtless / bare-chested. Some tattoos can be seen on the man's back when walking far behind the car on the street where there are hundreds of motorcycles.

3.

There is a wide garden planted on the whole roof. Three poles can be seen on top of the roof in the cloudy sky. The crowds are near under the eaves.

4.

The audience is paying attention to the show. There are four dancers holding red flags on the stage. One performer is playing with a circus ring in front of the audience.

5.

There is a bridge with three passengers in the middle of water. A weeping willow is at the end of the bridge. The woods are far behind the river bank.

6.

There are a flock of cranes behind the fence around the swampy yard. A crane stands still in the front.

7.

Three rhinos are under the shade of trees around them. They are resting in the yard and two of the rhinos are sleeping.

8.

The bridge connecting mountains stretches across the stream. The stream is far below the bridge in the middle of the valley.

9.

Some passengers are passing the suspension bridge with a red tower. There are rails by the sides of the cable-stayed bridge hung by two cables.

10.

Three swans are swimming and following four ducks. They are crossing the river under an arch bridge.

11.

Hot, beautiful, refreshing air drenches heavenly sandy beach. The breeze is touching every grain of sand. The sky is idyllic, blue and clear. The beautiful, big blue ocean's waves are crashing to the cliffs.

12.

The warm, golden sand runs between your toes with the gentle breeze. As you sit alone, you find gorgeous, shiny shells that have been washed into the shore by the rippling of the water.

Beach A has hot, beautiful, refreshing air drenching heavenly sands, while beach B carries warm, golden sand running between your toes with the gentle breeze. The breeze in beach A is touching every grain of sand because the sky is idyllic, blue and clear. In beach A, the beautiful, big blue ocean's waves are crashing to the cliffs; in beach B, as you sit alone, you find gorgeous, shiny shells that have been washed into the shore by the rippling of the water.

錄音檔 Week 2　Day 4 (Thursday)

MP3 19

1. A. It's cold and sunny today.
   B. They're looking at a view.
   C. They're wearing coats.
   D. There is a beautiful reflection in the water.

2. A. The boy has short hair.
   B. The man wears a hat.
   C. The girl has long hair.
   D. The boy wears a sport coat.

3. A. The cup is in front of the box.
   B. The red beans are filled inside the Dorayaki.
   C. A wallet is behind the box.
   D. There are flowers on the cup.

4. A. The statue is facing the girl.
   B. The girl is in front of the statue.
   C. The TV is far next to the statue.
   D. The TV is beyond the girl.

5. A. She's holding a scoop.

B. She's wearing a hood.

C. She's holding a plant.

D. She's planting a tree.

6. A. She's managing the plant.

    B. She's digging the ground.

    C. She's covering the dirt.

    D. She's spreading the soil.

7. A. They wear pants.

    B. They are watching behind.

    C. They wear sneakers.

    D. They wear raincoats.

8. A. Two buckets of water.

    B. They are all in T-shirts.

    C. Tools on the frames.

    D. Seven people.

9. A. There're signs in the front of the classroom.

    B. There's no teacher in the front of the classroom.

    C. On the front, you can see a black poster with signs.

    D. There're posters on the wall.

10. A. They're two beverage vending machines.

    B. There are two wooden zebras in back of the scooters.

    C. One of them is in front of the billboard.

    D. One of them is next to the trail.

11. A. There is a dog in the cages.

    B. The dog is in a vest.

    C. Part of the cages is made of wood.

    D. Part of the cages is made of steel.

12. A. He is looking at his left.

    B. He is looking at us.

    C. He is looking out.

    D. He is looking for company.

13. A. They are talking to each other.

    B. They are waiting to check in far from the counter.

    C. They are waiting to check in an airport.

    D. They are waiting behind the barricade tape.

14. A. The car gets stuck by the side, so traffic is moving very slowly.

B. The opposite side of the highway is cleared for the traffic accident.

C. The traffic is jammed at this time of the day.

D. There's been an accident. A car has just hit the rail.

15. A. We are approaching the station. Please get ready to alight.

B. When the doors are opened, please keep clear of the doors.

C. The train is arriving. Please get ready to board.

D. We are approaching the terminal station. Thank you for your patronage.

16. A. Our school basketball team won again.

B. It was a tough game last night.

C. Their players on the other team were much taller than ours,

D. but our offense and defense were much better.

17. A. A winter vacation is in Bali Island.

B. The weather is nice throughout the year.

C. You can get a nice tan.

D. Pack your swimsuit and sunglasses now.

MP3 20

Complete Description

1. It's cold and sunny today and they're in coats watching a view. There is a beautiful reflection in the water.

2. The boy has short hair and wears a sport coat. The man wears a hat and the girl next to him has long hair.

3. There is a box of Dorayaki filled with red beans. A cup with flowers is in front of the box. A wallet is behind the box.

4. The girl is worshiping the statue facing her. The TV is far away next to the statue beyond the girl.

5. The girl in a hood is holding a scoop in her right hand, and planting a small tree with her left hand.

6. The girl managing the plant is digging the ground, covering the dirt by spreading the soil.

7. The people behind the girl wearing pants and sneakers and raincoats are watching.

8. There are seven people in T-shirts in the room. Tools are on the frames on top of two buckets of water.

9. There're signs with black poster in the front of the classroom with posters on the wall. There's no teacher in the classroom.

10. Before two beverage vending machines, there are two wooden zebras in back of the scooters. One of them is in front of the billboard and the other is next to the trail.

11. There is a dog in a vest in the cages. The cages are made of wood and steel.

12. The dog is looking to his left at us, and he is looking out for company.

13. The two men talking to each other are waiting to check in far from the counter. They are waiting to check in an airport behind the barricade tape.

14. There's been an accident. The car has just hit the rail and got stuck by the side, so the traffic is moving very slowly. The opposite side of the highway is cleared for the traffic accident. The traffic is jammed at this time of the day.

15. We are approaching the station. Please get ready to alight. When the doors open, please keep clear of the doors. This is the terminal station. Thank you for your patronage. As for the departing passengers, when the train arrives, please get ready to board after all the arriving passengers alight.

16. Our school basketball team won the national title the fourth year in a row. The championship game was held last night. It was a tough game. The players on the other team were much taller than ours, but our offense and defense were much better and stronger. At the bottom of the last period, the score was tied. We felt very nervous as we watched the game. Then, our player Jeremy made a Three-point shot. The crowd cheered. We had won the game!

17. If you plan to take a vacation in winter, Bali Island in Indonesia is a great place to go. The weather is nice throughout the year, but the best time of the year is from December to April. It rains sometimes, but the rain can cool you off. You can get a nice tan. Imagine that you are enjoying the sunshine at the beach on the island while your friends are shivering in the cold at home. So, what are you waiting for? Pack your swimsuit and sunglasses for a wonderful vacation in the sun — here in Bali Island.

· ·

録音稿 **Week 2　Day 5 (Friday)**

MP3 21

Picture Description with Questions and Responses.

1. (A) What is the boy doing?
　 (B) What is the boy wearing?
　 (C) What is the girl doing?

   (D) What is the girl wearing?
2. (A) Where are the people?
   (B) What are the people doing?
   (C) What are the people wearing?
   (D) What are they waiting for?
3. (A) What does the girl wear?
   (B) What is the girl cooking with?
   (C) What is the girl stirring?
   (D) What do you think she is cooking?
4. (A) Where is the path leading to?
   (B) Have you been there before?
   (C) What are behind the waterfall?
   (D) How does it feel like in the waterfall?
5. (A) What are the trees made of?
   (B) What are the trees bound with?
   (C) What do you think the trees are for?
   (D) What are behind the trees?
6. (A) Where is the playground?
   (B) Where are the ladders leading to?
   (C) Have you played with the swings?
   (D) Why isn't there anybody?
7. (A) What is the stilt walker doing to the crowds?
   (B) What is the stilt walker holding?
   (C) What is the woman doing to him?
   (D) How are the crowds reacting?
8. (A) What is the statue wearing?
   (B) Is that Super Mario?
   (C) Why do they hold it on the street?
   (D) What are the people lifting him wearing?
9. (A) What is the woman doing?
   (B) What is the woman wearing?
   (C) What is the woman riding?
   (D) What is behind the woman?
10. (A) What are people playing behind the basketball stands?
   (B) Are they playing basketball?
   (C) What do you think the man standing by the basketball stands is doing?

(D) What are hanging above the court?

....

Answers
1. (A) The boy is crying.
   (B) The boy is wearing a cowboy hat.
   (C) The girl is smiling.
   (D) The girl is wearing a hat.
2. (A) The people are in an arcade by the classroom.
   (B) They are waiting for something.
   (C) They wear T-shirts.
   (D) They are waiting for the class.
3. (A) The girl wears an apron.
   (B) The girl is cooking with a pan.
   (C) The girl is stirring soup.
   (D) She is cooking vegetable soup.
4. (A) The path leads to the waterfall.
   (B) Yes. I have been there before.
   (C) A cave is behind the waterfall.
   (D) It feels like in a shower.
5. (A) The trees are made of bamboo.
   (B) The trees are bound with barrier tape.
   (C) I think the trees are a sign for gingko trees.
   (D) There are gingko trees behind the sign.
6. (A) The playground is in the woods.
   (B) The ladders lead to the woods.
   (C) Yes. I have played with the swings.
   (D) Because it is going to rain.
7. (A) The stilt walker is performing to the crowds.
   (B) The stilt walker is holding an umbrella.
   (C) The woman is taking a picture of him.
   (D) The crowds are paying attention on him.
8. (A) The statue wears suspender trousers.
   (B) Yes. It is Super Mario.
   (C) They hold it on the street for a parade.
   (D) The people lifting him are wearing diapers.

9. (A) The woman is on a parade.
   (B) The woman is wearing a fancy hat.
   (C) The woman is riding a float.
   (D) A classical Chinese building is behind the woman.
10. (A) The people are gathering behind the basketball stand.
   (B) No. They are not playing basketball.
   (C) The man standing by the basketball stands is waiting for his children.
   (D) There are banners hanging on the court.

錄音稿 Week 3 Day 1 (Monday)

MP3 23

above, against, among, at , at the back of, at the end (bottom) of, atop, before, behind, below, beneath, between, by, close to, in, inside, in front of, near, next to, on, on top of, over, under

MP3 24

A.

cleaning, crossing, cutting, drawing, drinking, eating, following, holding, jogging, listening, loading, locking, looking, making, packing, playing, pouring, pulling, pushing, selling, setting, sitting, speaking, stretching, sweeping, talking, typing, walking, watching, watering, working, wrapping, writing

B.

being-cleaned, cleared, displayed, dug up, handed, locked, painted, planted, poled, pilled, served, set up, towed, walked, washed, watered, wrapped

MP3 25

A.

afraid, asleep, beautiful, bent, bright, clean, dark, dirty, empty, flat, full, happy, heavy, high, light, long, open, rainy, round, tall, sad, straight, wet

B.

arranged, blocked, broken, chained, cleared, closed, crowded, crushed, deserted, displayed, equipped, loaded, occupied, parked, piled, posted, scattered, seated, stacked, stranded, tried

MP3 26

A.

afford / offer, awful / oval, ball / bawl, bike / hike, cheer / chair, clean / lean, coach / couch / , hitting / fitting, just / adjust, lake / rake, lamp / ramp, law / raw, lean / learn, light / right, lock / rock, low / row, owl / foul, mail / rail, meal / wheal, on the / under, peach / speech, peel / pill, pine / fine, player / prayer, playing / plane, pool / pull, poor / four, possible / impossible, rag / bag, selling / sailing, sheer / share, shopping / chopping, talk / take, there / they're, try / tie, wait / weigh, walk / work, west / rest, wheel / will

B.

aboard / abroad / board, inboard / onboard, agree / disagree, appear / disappear, aware / unaware, close / enclose, extract / exhale, just / adjust, relay / delay, reread / relayed, rest / arrest, similar / dissimilar, terrible / terrific, tie / untie, tire / retire, type / retype, underworked / underused, undrinkable / unthinkable

••

MP3 27

1. The dining table is under the lamp.
2. The two chairs are at the table.
3. The books are at the bottom of the shelf.
4. There is a bowl of flowers in the middle of the table.
5. There is a couch behind the table.
6. The girl is standing at the drum.
7. The man in a red cape is beneath the float.
8. The man in a black coat is in back of the float.
9. The boy is standing by the drums.
10. The two women on the bench are sitting by the road.

••

MP3 28

1. The two women sitting on the bench are watching the parade.
2. The girl is playing the drum.
3. The man in a red coat is walking by the float.
4. The man in a black coat is crossing the road.
5. The parade is stretching its length.
6. The man in a red cape is looking up to the float.
7. The last float is following the other float.

8. The boy by the drum is sweeping the floor with his foot.

9. The audiences of the parade are scattered along the road.

10. There are drums arranged for the tourists.

* * *

MP3 29

1. With light shedding from the window, the book room is bright.

2. The top of the book shelf is empty.

3. Without any lamps, the living room will be dark.

4. The parade is equipped with floats.

5. The road is occupied by the parade.

6. The audiences of the parade are not crowded.

7. The two women watching the parade are seated.

8. The bottom of the book shelf is full.

9. The table, bench, and couch in the living room are all long and straight.

10. The floors in both rooms are clean.

* * *

錄音稿 Week 3 Day2 (Tuesday)

MP3 30

1. There is a court in front of a shop or restaurant.

   There are many tables in the yard.

   The tables are covered with blue tablecloths.

   The tables are empty.

   There are parasols by the tables.

   The court is behind a tree with a lamp.

   There are plants scattered around the yard.

   There are two men sitting on the balcony behind the black banner.

   There are wooden rails around the balcony.

   There are fans on the ceiling of the balcony.

   The men sitting on the balcony is wearing white cap.

   There are no customers in the court.

2. The shirtless / bare-chested man is walking between the white line and guiding tile trail.

   The two women standing ahead of the man are looking outside at the side.

   Far ahead of them is a blue car on the road.

   There are hundreds of motorcycles parked along the left side of the road.

   The motorcycles are parked along the wall.

A long row of trees are shading the sidewalk by the wall.

The shirtless / bare-chested man has tattoos on his back.

There are red parasols on the right side of the road.

There is a green sign saying "Free..." next to the parasols.

3. There is a garden of roof across the square.

A crowd of people are gathering on the square.

There are three empty poles on top of the roof.

The garden is planted with different colors of flowers.

The whole garden is designed as rainbows across the sky.

The garden of rainbows is under a cloudy sky.

The crowds are entering the building.

The crowds are approaching the building's eaves.

4. There are four performers on the stage.

There are four dancers holding red flags on the stage.

The stage is in front of a Chinese classical building.

It's winter with a cloudy day.

There is a performer playing with circus rings in the square.

The audience is paying attention to the entertainment.

5. The bridge is in the middle of water.

There is a backpack girl by the rail in the center of the bridge.

There is a weeping willow at the end of the bridge.

A couple is facing the weeping willow.

The woods are far across the road by the river bank.

There are venders under the woods.

- -

錄音稿 Week 3 Day3 (Wednesday)

MP3 31

1. There are three passers on the bridge.

The suspension bridge has a red tower.

The bridge is leading to a foothill / bottom of a mountain.

The bridge is hung by two cables.

There are rails by the sides of the cable-stayed bridge.

The rails are linked with wires / wire mesh.

2. Three swans are swimming across the river.

The swans are following the four ducks ahead of them.

The other two ducks are in the wake of the swans.

There is an arch bridge over the river.

Two passers are watching the flocks.

A string of small banners is under the bridge.

The lake has a reflection of the vegetation deeply embedding the whole picture.

3. 1). This is a beach with hot, beautiful, refreshing air.

2). Ocean waves lap the sand on the beach.

3). The breeze is touching every grain of sand.

4). The sky is idyllic, blue and clear.

5). The beautiful, big blue ocean's waves are crashing to the cliffs.

6). Hot, beautiful, refreshing air drenches heavenly sandy beach. The breeze is touching every grain of sand. The sky is idyllic, blue and clear. The beautiful, big blue ocean's waves are crashing to the cliffs.

4. 1). The warm, golden sands run through your toes.

2). The gentle breeze is warmly stroking your face.

3). You sit alone in the bosom of the ocean.

4). You find gorgeous, shiny shells rolling in the waves.

5). The shells have been washed into the shore by the rippling of the water.

6). The warm, golden sand runs between your toes with the gentle breeze. As you sit alone, you find gorgeous, shiny shells that have been washed into the shore by the rippling of the water.

∙∙

錄音稿 Week 3 Day4 (Thursday)

MP3 32

1. It's a cold and sunny day.

They're looking at a view.

They're wearing coats.

There is a beautiful reflection in the water.

The boy has short hair.

The man wears a cap.

The girl has long hair.

The boy wears a sport coat.

It's a cold and sunny day and they're in coats looking at a view. There is a beautiful reflection in the water. The boy has short hair and wears sport coat. The man wears a hat and the girl next to him has long hair.

2. The cup is in front of the box.
   The red beans are filled inside the Dorayaki.
   A wallet is behind the box.
   There are flowers on the cup.
   There is a box of Dorayaki filled with red beans. A cup with flowers is in front of the box. A wallet is behind the box.

3. Three rhinos are under the shade of palm trees.
   The weeds are behind the rhinos.
   They are resting in the yard.
   There is a bunker with iron bars at the rear of the yard.
   Two of the rhinos are sleeping.

4. The bridge connects mountains.
   The bridge stretches across the stream.
   The stream comes down from deep inside of mountains.
   The stream passes through the green, shady valley.
   The stream is far below the bridge.
   The branches of trees leans forward the center of the stream.
   The bridge is in the middle of the valley.

∙∙∙

錄音檔 Week3 Day 5 (Friday)
MP3 33
1. (A) Where is the path leading to?
      The path leads to the waterfall.
   (B) Have you been there before?
      Yes. I have been there before.
   (C) What are behind the waterfall?
      A cave is behind the waterfall.
   (D) How does it feel like in the waterfall?
      It feels like in a shower.
2. (A) What are the trees made of?
      The trees are made of bamboo.
   (B) What are the trunks bound with?
      The trunks are bound with barrier tape.
   (C) What do you think the trees are for?

I think the trees are a sign for gingko trees.

    (D) What are behind the trees?

      There are gingko trees behind the sign.

3. (A) Where is the playground?

      The playground is in the woods.

    (B) Where are the ladders leading to?

      The ladders lead to the woods.

    (C) Have you played with the swings?

      Yes. I have played with the swings.

    (D) Why isn't there anybody?

      Because it is going to rain.

4. (A) What is the stilt walker doing to the crowds?

      The stilt walker is performing to the crowds.

    (B) What is the stilt walker holding?

      The stilt walker is holding an umbrella.

    (C) What is the woman doing to him?

      The woman is taking a picture of him.

    (D) How are the crowds reacting?

      The crowds are paying attention on him.

錄音稿 Week 4 Day 1 (Monday)

MP3 34

1. Would you mind typing in this letter, please?

    (A) Yes, please.

    (B) I haven't seen it before.

    (C) No, not at all.

2. How long have you been living here?

    (A) Since 2001.

    (B) I like living here.

    (C) I always live here.

3. What does he look like?

    (A) He looks alive.

    (B) A doctor or a lawyer.

    (C) Right.

4. How about going to the movie?.

    (A) Good idea!

(B) Go straight to the right.

(C) We couldn't.

5. Could I have a look at the menu, please?

(A) OK. Here you are.

(B) Oh, it's new!

(C) Why not?

6. Do you have any luggage, sir?

(A) Wish me luck.

(B) Just this one suitcase.

(C) Did you see my baggage?

7. I'd like to speak to the manager, please.

(A) Why can't you speak?

(B) You can manage.

(C) I'm sorry. She's not here.

8. I like soccer game seasons.

(A) So do I.

(B) Neither do you.

(C) Me either.

9. May I see your driving license, please?

(A) Yes, you will.

(B) Of course.

(C) I pass it.

10. Could I speak to Mr. Snow, please?

(A) I'll put you through to his secretary now, sir.

(B) I'll hold.

(C) Yes. My name's Snow.

MP3 35

1. Would you mind typing in this letter, please?
   No, not at all.

2. How long have you been living here?
   Since 2001.

3. What does he look like?
   A doctor or a lawyer.

4. How about going to the movie?
   Good idea!

5. Could I have a look at the menu, please?
   OK. Here you are.
6. Do you have any luggage, sir?
   Just this one suitcase.
7. I'd like to speak to the manager, please.
   I'm sorry. She's not here.
8. I like soccer game seasons.
   So do I.
9. May I see your driving license, please?
   Of course.
10. Could I speak to Mr. Snow, please?
    I'll put you through to his secretary now, sir.

錄音稿 Week 4 Day 2 (Tuesday)

MP3 36

1. How are you doing?
   (A) Just fine, thanks.
   (B) So am I.
   (C) They're doing home.
   (D) No, I do nothing.
2. Where did you live?
   (A) Some fruits.
   (B) Every morning.
   (C) Two months ago.
   (D) In Taipei.
3. Let's go to see a movie tonight.
   (A) Well, he's out now.
   (B) Sorry, I'm busy tonight.
   (C) Sure, I'll make it up.
   (D) Yeah, I think it's a good story.
4. Who's Jennifer watching now?
   (A) In the next door.
   (B) Right after the movie.
   (C) About the story.
   (D) Her boyfriend, I think.
5. I heard John made it better today.

(A) It's close to the bus stop.

(B) There's a museum near here.

(C) Usually at 5, except for Sunday.

(D) It's open every day.

6. Have you ever been to Ali Mountain before?

(A) Yes, I went there last year.

(B) Yes, I've seen it once.

(C) No, I don't know where it is.

(D) No, I wasn't there.

7. Sorry, I've got to run now. May I call you back tonight?

(A) No. Mary is on another line.

(B) Sure, I'll be in my office until 5.

(C) All right. Call it off.

(D) Yes, please.

8. When does the museum open on weekdays?

(A) That's good news.

(B) But I like this one better.

(C) Oh, I'm glad he's better.

(D) Yeah, I've asked his mother.

9. You are two days behind on your deadline.

(A) I'll move to the line.

(B) Really? Where is the line?

(C) I'm sorry. I'll put it on your desk tomorrow.

(D) I won't cross the line.

10. Honestly, I don't think Jenny's idea will work.

(A) She starts tomorrow.

(B) I like her idea, too.

(C) She is idle today.

(D) Neither do I.

11. Excuse me, is there a parking lot in this neighborhood?

(A) Yes, you may be excused.

(B) Yes, there's one on the next corner.

(C) Yes, it belongs to my neighbors.

(D) Yes, this is Park Road.

12. How would you like your steak?

(A) I'd like to stay.

(B) I'm going to take it.

(C) I love to play football.

(D) Medium, please.

13. Do you plan to major in History in college?

(A) Yes, I'll give him a tour of the college.

(B) No, I want to be an English major.

(C) No, I went to college in Taiwan.

(D) Yes, most of my friends joined a club.

14. This coat is a bit tight. Could I try on a larger size?

(A) Yes, you could try this room.

(B) Well, the color is too dark.

(C) No, there're no mice.

(D) Certainly. One moment, please.

15. Oh, my goodness! I just can't remember where I put my ticket.

(A) Sorry, I don't have a ticket.

(B) You got 70 tickets, remember?

(C) Didn't you put it in your pocket?

(D) Sure, I'll tick it on the form.

∙∙

MP3 37

Activity One

A.

(ASK) : Am I late?

(ANSWER) : Yes, you are. (OR) No, you are not.

(ASK) : Are you a student

(ANSWER) : Yes, I am. (OR) No, I am not.

(ASK) : Is he on vacation?

(ANSWER) : Yes, he is. (OR) No, he isn't.

(ASK) : Was he your teacher?

(ANSWER) : Yes, he was. (OR) No, he wasn't.

(ASK) : Were you scared?

(ANSWER) : Yes, I was. (OR) No, I wasn't.

B.

(ASK) : Do you like watching TV?

(ANSWER) : Yes, I do. (OR) No, I don't.

(ASK) : Does she smoke?

(ANSWER) : Yes she does. (OR) No, she doesn't.
(ASK) : Did you do the dish?
(ANSWER) : Yes I did. (OR) No, I didn't.
(ASK) : Can you ride the bicycle?
(ANSWER) : Yes I can. (OR) No, I can't.
(ASK) : May I come to visit you?
(ANSWER) : Yes you may. (OR) No, you may not.
(ASK) : Will you buy the car?
(ANSWER) : Yes, I will. (OR) No, I won't.
(ASK) : Should I give her some money?
(ANSWER) : Yes, you should. (OR) No, you shouldn't.
(ASK) : Would you be quiet?
(ANSWER) : Yes, I would. (OR) No, I wouldn't.
(ASK) : Might I see him just once more!
(ANSWER) : Yes, you might. (OR) No, you might never see him again.
(ASK) : Have you cleaned the floor?
(ANSWER) : Yes, I have. (OR) No, I haven't.
(ASK) : Has he made the promise?
(ANSWER) : Yes, he has. (OR) No, he hasn't.

MP3 38

Activity Two

1. How are you doing? Just fine, thanks.

2. Where did you live? In Taipei.

3. Let's go to see a movie tonight. Sorry, I'm busy tonight.

4. Who's Jennifer watching at now? Her boyfriend, I think.

5. I heard John made it better today. Oh, that's a good news.

6. Have you ever been to Ali Mountain before?
   Yes, I went there last year.

7. Sorry, I've got to run now. May I call you back tonight?
   Sure, I'll be in my office until 5.

8. When does the museum open on weekdays?
   It's usually at 5, except for Sunday.

9. You are two days behind on your deadline.
   I'm sorry. I'll put it on your desk tomorrow.

10. Honestly, I don't think Jenny's idea will work.

Neither do I.

11. Excuse me, is there a parking lot in this neighborhood?

Yes, there's one on the next corner.

12. How would you like your steak?

Medium, please.

13. Do you plan to major in History in college?

No, I want to be an English major.

14. This coat is a bit tight. Could I try on a larger size?

Certainly. Just a moment, please.

15. Oh, my goodness! I just can't remember where I put my ticket.

Didn't you put it in your pocket?

錄音稿 Week 4 Day 3 (Wednesday)

MP3 39

1. What time do you get to work every day?

(A) Many days.

(B) Earlier than 8:30.

(C) I don't get it.

2. Is he back from work yet?

(A) He is back!

(B) He is not bad at all.

(C) Not yet.

3. Where should I get the file?

(A) You should have.

(B) Ask the secretary.

(C) I'd like a cup of coffee.

4. I've got a problem.

(A) What is it?

(B) It's likely a problem.

(C) Maybe you have got it.

5. Do you watch the TV news every day?

(A) Which news?

(B) I like watching news.

(C) Yes, I do.

6. What do you think of this painting?

(A) The first one or the second one?

 (B) I don't feel like painting it.

 (C) I think so.

7. I am afraid you have the wrong phone number.

 (A) Yes, you are.

 (B) Yes, I'm wrong.

 (C) Oh, I'm sorry.

8. Can you tell me which way south is?

 (A) Why not?

 (B) It's that way.

 (C) North.

9. You can't have my laptop. You'll lose it.

 (A) I won't get lost.

 (B) I promise I won't.

 (C) Trust me. I will win.

10. It's an emergency. Could you put me through to the police, please?

 (A) What emergency?

 (B) They're not busy at the moment.

 (C) I'll put you through right now.

MP3 40

1. What time do you get to work every day?
   Earlier than 8:30.

2. Is he back from work yet?
   Not yet.

3. Where should I get the file?
   Ask the secretary.

4. I've got a problem.
   What is it?

5. Do you watch the TV news every day?
   Yes, I do.

6. What do you think of this painting?
   The first one or the second one?

7. I am afraid you have the wrong phone number.
   Oh, I'm sorry.

8. Can you tell me which way south is?
   It's that way.

9. You can't have my laptop. You'll lose it.

   I promise I won't.

10. It's an emergency. Could you put me through to the police, please?

    I'll put you through right now.

••

錄音稿 Week 4　Day 4 (Thursday)

MP3 41

1. Do you know how to operate the machine?

   (A) That's right.

   (B) Sure. I'll operate it.

   (C) Let me show you.

2. What's your schedule like yesterday?

   (A) I really like it.

   (B) It's hustle and bustle.

   (C) They are scheduled to arrive yesterday.

3. Before you write a report, first of all, select your topic.

   (A) OK, what's next?

   (B) Everybody ought to read it.

   (C) Can I report after that?

4. If you find something wrong, just cross it out.

   (A) What if I think it's right?

   (B) Is it just across from the river?

   (C) Then they should cross the street.

5. The sign indicates the room for the meeting.

   (A) Oh, thanks.

   (B) So, do I need to sign here?

   (C) I'm not sure how to meet one.

6. Can you turn down the TV?

   (A) But I can hardly hear it!

   (B) The louder, the better.

   (C) Please don't turn me down.

7. How come you always come to class so early?

   (A) No, not really.

   (B) They usually start at 8:00.

   (C) I never stay up late.

8. Have you ever taken lessons before?
   (A) Yes, a long time ago.
   (B) Yes, with a prison.
   (C) Sure, I love this song.
9. What do you think of the music?
   (A) I think of it all the time.
   (B) It's soothing.
   (C) I can't think of the name.
10. Do you recognize this love song?
   (A) That's amazing!
   (B) I've never heard it before.
   (C) It's such a lovely song!

....

MP3 42

1. Do you know how to operate the machine?
   Let me show you.
2. What's your schedule like yesterday?
   It's hustle and bustle.
3. Before you write a report, first of all, select your topic.
   OK, what's next?
4. If you find something wrong, just cross it out.
   What if I think it's right?
5. The sign indicates the room for the meeting.
   Oh, thanks.
6. Can you turn down the TV?
   But I can hardly hear it!
7. How come you always come to class so early?
   I never stay up late.
8. Have you ever taken lessons before?
   Yes, a long time ago.
9. What do you think of the music?
   It's soothing.
10. Do you recognize this love song?
   I've never heard it before.

....

錄音稿 Week 4 Day 5 (Friday)

MP3 43

Mark your answer on your answer sheet.

1. Do you have any idea where our team is?
   (A) Let's invite them here.
   (B) That's a great idea!
   (C) The one in blue.

2. Which one is his?
   (A) Let me hear the one.
   (B) He won.
   (C) Let me see them.

3. How well do you think we will do?
   (A) Actually, I will think.
   (B) We will be hard to beat.
   (C) We may go swimming.

4. Who is this present for?
   (A) It's six, not four.
   (B) It could be for Tom.
   (C) That's the present.

5. A lot of players are on the field!
   (A) Some of them will play.
   (B) They are not feeling well.
   (C) Why don't we play against each other?

6. As chairman, I'd like to call this meeting to order.
   (A) You have my order.
   (B) But Bill and Sue are not here yet.
   (C) You should have called them.

7. Who is the treasurer of the corporation?
   (A) I don't know.
   (B) My colleague is a real treasure.
   (C) We treasure your talent.

8. You must be thrilled on a roll.
   (A) You are here. Let's call the roll!
   (B) I just hit my winning streak.
   (C) Yes, the egg rolls are delicious.

9. Secretarial job is my least favorite work of all!

    (A) That's a secret.

    (B) My favorite, too!

    (C) What else can you do?

10. What if no people join us?

    (A) I doubt that will happen.

    (B) The joins are hardly seen.

    (C) They joined the club too.

···

MP3 44

Team Activity

1. Do you have any idea where our team is?

    The one in blue.

2. Which one is his?

    Let me see them.

3. How well do you think we will do?

    We will be hard to beat.

4. Who is this present for?

    It could be for Tom.

5. A lot of players are on the field!

    Some of them will play.

Meetings

6. As chairman, I'd like to call this meeting to order.

    But Bill and Sue are not here yet.

7. Who is the treasurer of the corporation?

    I don't know.

8. You must be thrilled on a roll.

    I just hit my winning streak.

9. Secretarial job is my least favorite work of all!

    What else can you do?

10. What if no people join us?

    I doubt that will happen.

Leader 038

拯救你的英檢聽力！四週勇闖英語檢定(MP3)

作　　　者	常安陸
發 行 人	周瑞德
執行總監	齊心瑀
企劃編輯	劉俞青
執行編輯	陳韋佑、魏于婷
校　　　對	編輯部
封面構成	高鍾琪

內文照片	Apple Daily http://www.appledaily.com.tw/realtimenews/article/new/20150816/670913/、Grayn Wu
內頁構成	華漢電腦排版有限公司
印　　　製	大亞彩色印刷製版股份有限公司
初　　　版	2016 年 2 月
定　　　價	新台幣 380 元
出　　　版	力得文化
電　　　話	(02) 2351-2007
傳　　　真	(02) 2351-0887
地　　　址	100 台北市中正區福州街 1 號 10 樓之 2
E - m a i l	best.books.service@gmail.com
網　　　址	www.bestbookstw.com

港澳地區總經銷	泛華發行代理有限公司
地　　　址	香港新界將軍澳工業邨駿昌街 7 號 2 樓
電　　　話	(852) 2798-2323
傳　　　真	(852) 2796-5471

國家圖書館出版品預行編目資料

拯救你的英檢聽力!四週勇闖英語檢定 / 常安陸著. --
初版. -- 臺北市 : 力得文化, 2016.02
　面 ;　　公分. --（Leader ; 38）
ISBN 978-986-92398-8-2(平裝附光碟片)

1.英語 2.讀本

805.1892　　　　　　104029312